SHADOW'S CAPTIVE

SHADOW ISLAND SERIES: BOOK TWO

MARY STONE

LORI RHODES

An estimated 460,000 children go missing in the U.S. each year. This book is dedicated in memory and in honor of those who are lost and those who miss them deeply.

DESCRIPTION

Want a puppy, little girl?

Former FBI agent Rebecca West came to Shadow Island to relax and clear her head, not step into a dead sheriff's long worn shoes. Here she is, though, Interim Sheriff over a small department grieving for their boss and friend.

But not for long.

Before she can resign from the unwanted position, a little girl goes missing. On vacation with her parents, the eight-year-old was last seen outside her family's vacation rental drawing on the sidewalk with a box of chalk.

Now she's gone.

Did the girl wander off and get lost or maybe pulled out by the tide? Was she lured away? Or has she become the victim of something more sinister on Shadow Island, where a darkness simmers just below the paradisiacal surface?

When Rebecca discovers two similar abductions nearby within the week, she fears the worst. With a lot of ground to cover, few deputies to help, and the events surrounding Sheriff Wallace's death haunting them all, can Rebecca and her team find the young girls before it's too late?

From the gripping beginning to the startling conclusion, Shadow's Captive—the second book in the Shadow Island Series by Mary Stone and Lori Rhodes—will ensure you always know where your children are.

1

Today was going to be the best day of her life. Sylvie just knew it. Even if it was starting off to be a snooze-fest of epic proportions.

"*Heavenly girth on an onion slice, not too many pickles, and not precise.*"

In spite of how annoyed she was at the delay of the best day of her life, Sylvie giggled as her dad's voice rumbled from the kitchen. Dad was real good at a lot of things, like building sandcastles and playing monsters so she could stomp them flat. But "he couldn't carry a tune in a bucket." At least, that's what Sylvie's momma always said.

Even at eight years and ten months old, she knew her dad was singing "Cheeseburger in Paradise" all wrong. How did she know? 'Cause he played it over and over and over in the car whenever they drove to the beach, and he hadn't stopped belting it out at random ever since.

He'd done it different enough each time that she was pretty sure he didn't even try to remember the words. With the way he and Momma would crack up as he messed them up, however, she was pretty sure he was doing it on purpose.

Dad was standing at the stove—now that he'd finally woken up—scrambling some eggs while drinking his first cup of coffee. Sylvie had been up for hours already. There was a whole beach out there waiting for them, and her parents had decided to sleep in? Didn't they know that vacation time was all about having fun?

Where was the fun in staying in bed after the sun came up? There were waves to chase and pretty shells to put in her special glass jar. The ocean was just a few streets away. And where was she?

Stuck here...waiting in agony.

It was awful. She'd waited all winter long and the whole spring too. She'd even waited 'til school let out for the year. Now she had to wait some more for her dad to have his breakfast.

Shnookerdookies!

Smiling as she thought of her favorite curse word, Sylvie took in a long breath, knowing she shouldn't really complain. Being here might not have happened at all. She'd heard her parents talk about something called a "budget" and how a trip would "blow their budget to smithereens."

She hadn't known what that meant, but from the tone of their voices, Sylvie knew it wasn't good.

Then things had gotten better, and Sylvie had been so excited when Dad told her the thrilling news. They were going on this trip because he'd gotten paid from "overtime." She didn't know where "overtime" was located or what kind of job it was, but apparently it paid more than using his blowtorch to weld stuff. It also made him work longer hours, and it had been forever since they'd been able to spend any real time together.

Totally worth it!

She'd spent the last two days, the whole time, hanging out

and playing with him and Momma. It had been the best two days of her life.

They'd eaten sandwiches and ice cream, splashed in the water, chased seagulls, and played in the sand. They'd had so much time together that she'd gotten to tell him all about her friends. She'd fallen asleep on the couch last night watching movies but woke up in her bed this morning.

Now, she was eager to do it all again.

Sylvie's eyes had popped open as soon as the sun lit up her window, ready to start another day of fun and adventures. She'd thrown on her favorite swimsuit, even though it was still a little damp from the day before. It had been a struggle to put on, but Sylvie wasn't going to wait for Momma to wake up.

She figured the sooner she got ready, the less there'd be for Momma to do, so they could get out of the little rental in a flash. Momma wouldn't have to worry about gathering Sylvie's toys and other beach stuff, because Sylvie wanted to prove how grown-up she was and do it herself.

Using a pink scrunchie, she'd brushed her hair back into a high ponytail that was only a little crooked. She'd even dug through the big rainbow-striped bag and found the sunscreen Momma had insisted she wear on every inch of her skin. It was hard. Not as hard as putting on a wet swimsuit, but she managed to do it all on her own. After all, she was a big girl now.

So big that I can go to the beach by myself?

"Just because we're on vacation doesn't mean the rules don't apply anymore." Momma was always talking about the rules.

But then Dad had bought her a candy apple before their pizza dinner. So maybe some rules didn't apply when the sand was so near.

It was so tempting, but nope. She'd already been lectured a billion times to "never, ever leave the yard by herself."

Which was why she was sitting there in total agony, waiting.

Turning to see the big clock on the bedroom wall, Sylvie struggled to read the dang thing. Why couldn't the world just accept that life was digital and stop with the old stuff already?

Little hand on the ten and big hand on the six. Ten thirty.

Ugh. Ugh. Ugh.

That meant the day was practically gone.

Tiptoeing down the short hall, Sylvie peeked into her parents' bedroom again. Momma was still sleeping. It made Sylvie want to scream.

She didn't, of course, because she was "the best daughter in the whole wide world" and didn't want to lose the rep. But really?

Tiptoeing back to the kitchen, Sylvie watched her dad still cooking at the stove. Couldn't he just have cereal and juice like she did hours ago?

Plus, he wasn't even ready. For some reason, he had put on normal clothes instead of his beach stuff. He had on a t-shirt and his shorts with all the pockets, which was what he wore back home every day. That just didn't make any sense to Sylvie.

Maybe all the sun had shrunk their brains?

Tired of waiting for her parents to realize what a beautiful day it was, Sylvie wandered over to the box of toys and started digging. This wasn't her toy box from home. She'd peeked inside when they'd first arrived but had been too busy having fun to investigate it more fully.

It had to have something good inside, she reasoned.

She found dolls and cars and trucks and coloring books with most of the pages scribbled on. None of those looked interesting, though. Those were inside toys, for when the rain came or for at night when it was too scary to play in the ocean. After just a few more moments of digging, Sylvie found the perfect toy to pass the time.

Clutching the prize, she turned and raced into the kitchen. "Dad, I'm gonna go decorate the sidewalk."

"You're going to what?" Her father stopped singing and looked away from the skillet. She showed him the box of sidewalk chalk she'd found. Thankfully, he nodded and waved his egg-caked spatula at the window over the sink. "Oh, okay, baby girl. Just make sure you stay in front of the house where I can see you. Once I'm done eating and get cleaned up, we can go down to the beach and let your momma sleep in some more."

Sylvie nodded, grabbed her treasure, and finally ran into the sunshine. Being stuck inside all day was nearly as bad as being at school. The sun was up, but it wasn't too hot yet. It was the perfect time to play in the yard. And unlike their house, this one had a pale gray sidewalk that would be perfect to draw on.

In short order, she was sprawled on her belly, doing her best to draw that cheeseburger from paradise Dad kept singing about. Hopefully, he would see it and remember the rest of the words to the song. She colored the orange cheese and green lettuce.

She was fully caught up in drawing her purple hamburger bun when a little whimper caught her attention. The soft noise sent a jolt up her spine. The neighborhood had been quiet all morning long, except for the seagulls. Looking up, she caught sight of something even better than a beach full of pretty shells.

A fluffy, golden-furred puppy was heading down the sidewalk toward her. His tiny ears bobbed with each step. He was sniffing along the ground at the edge of the sidewalk. Sylvie had to clap both hands over her mouth to contain her squeal of excitement.

Momma said puppies didn't like to be squealed at. Puppies were baby dogs, so she had to be nice and gentle with them so she wouldn't scare or hurt the sweet little balls of fur.

With slow and careful movements, Sylvie stood and made her way over to where the puppy was, just a few houses down. As she got close, the puppy noticed her. His tail wagged as he trotted up.

Tucking one chalk piece into the swimsuit strap on her shoulder, Sylvie bent over and held her hand out flat, just like she'd been taught. The little fluff ball inspected it for a moment, giving her a few sniffs. She couldn't hold back her squeal of happiness as he started licking her toes.

Setting another piece of chalk down on the sidewalk, she stroked his soft fur. "What are you doing out here, little puppy? Where's your momma?" Sylvie glanced around but didn't see any other dogs in the area. There was just an old ugly van parked down the street, but that was it. There weren't even any other people around.

Everyone was probably at the beach already.

Maybe the reason I'm not at the beach right now too is because I'm supposed to save this puppy.

As the thought took hold, Sylvie gathered the dog up into her arms and giggled as the little guy gave her kisses all over her cheeks. "I can't just leave you here on your own. You're just a baby dog." He wasn't wearing a collar, and every pet that had an owner wore a collar, she knew. That meant he wasn't anyone's pet yet, right?

A wonderful idea took hold of Sylvie's mind. *Yes!*

"Maybe if I take you back with me, Momma will let me keep you." Sylvie was, after all, only one year and two months away from her tenth birthday, so she knew she was old enough to have a puppy of her very own. Struggling to keep her grip on the wiggly body, which was heavier than she'd expected, Sylvie turned and headed back toward their little rental house.

Now she needed to come up with some good arguments to convince her parents to let her keep this precious puppy. He clearly already loved her because he kept licking her while wagging his tail.

"If Daddy keeps working at Overtime, I could at least have you to play with me. And if he doesn't, then we can all play together! Are you hungry, baby? Dad's making eggs. Do you like eggs?"

"Goldie! Where'd you go, boy? Goldie."

Sylvie froze in front of the neighbor's house. With wide, guilty eyes, she stared down at the golden puppy in her arms. He started writhing as if trying to get away.

Oh no.

"Excuse me, little girl, have you seen a golden retriever puppy around here?"

Her head hanging low with embarrassment, and feeling ashamed for taking something that wasn't hers, Sylvie turned to show the man what she was holding.

"I'm sorry, mister." She realized she was whispering and raised her voice so he could hear her from so far away. "I...I thought he was lost." Sylvie snuggled into the soft fur under her chin, not ready to say goodbye. "I was gonna take him home to Momma to see what I should do."

The man laughed, but not in a mean way. He was tall and bald, and with his back to the sun, Sylvie couldn't get a good look at his face.

"Oh, he was for a minute there. Thankfully, you were able to find him for me. Can you bring him back, please? I need to take him and the rest of his littermates down to the surf shop. I'm giving them away."

That perked Sylvie up, and she lifted her head. He was giving them away? Maybe she could keep him after all. Still holding the puppy, she walked back down the sidewalk. He was across the street, waiting by the ugly old van she'd seen earlier. It wasn't the first time she'd seen the van. Was he one of the neighbors or a visitor like her?

"You're giving them away? Does that mean for free?"

The man opened the long, rolling passenger door and gestured inside. "Yep, my old bitch, Tammy, had a whole litter."

Sylvie gaped at the man, shocked at how easily the bad word had rolled out of his mouth. It wasn't a really, really bad word, though. Female dogs were called bitches, or so Dad said.

"How many do you have?"

The nice man smiled. "Too many to keep." He chuckled. "There are so many of them, it's hard to get them all in at the same time. That's how that little rascal got away."

Yips and barks came from the back of the van, and Sylvie's excitement grew. "I love puppies."

The nice man patted the side of the van. "Would you like to see them?"

Sylvie couldn't contain her laughter. "Yes, please!"

She knew she wasn't supposed to cross the street on her own, but she also knew her momma would be proud of her for returning the puppy to his owner. Maybe even proud enough to allow her to keep one of them.

After looking both ways, up and down the street like she'd been taught, she scampered across. The black road was hot on her feet, so she ran as fast as she could. If she could be quiet and fast, Dad wouldn't even know she'd left the yard.

She barely even looked at the man. He was busy unfolding a blanket and not paying her any attention at all. Rushing to the open door, she peered inside.

It was the weirdest van Sylvie had ever seen. There were no seats in the back, and a black wall blocked off the front seats. Even stranger, all of the windows were coated with something like black paint, so no light came in. It was dark, and Sylvie struggled to see after being out in the sun for so long.

There was some kind of fabric, like the blanket the man was holding, crumpled up on the floor with a small black rectangle on it. It was smaller than a phone, and she could hear the sounds of puppies coming from it.

That was weird.

The pile of cloth didn't seem big enough to hide a pack of puppies, though. Leaning in while trying not to squish Goldie, she peered into the back to see if they were hiding there.

"It's okay, puppies. I brought your brother back." She did her best to whistle, but it didn't work quite right.

Before she could get any of the puppies to come out of hiding, a black cloth came down and covered her head. Arms wrapped around her sides, pinning her arms down, squishing her and the puppy. He let out a squeak. She was jerked off her feet and into the air. Before she could do anything, or even think, a hand clamped down over her mouth.

Goldie yelped and kicked, trying to get free. She tried to un-squish him but couldn't push away the one arm that was still holding them both so tight.

Like a flash of lightning, Sylvie became terrified. Her high-pitched whimper joined the puppy's. It was dark inside the blanket, and she didn't like it. She tried to kick and wriggle, but she was completely tangled up in the heavy fabric and could barely move. All the sounds were muffled, like when Momma and Dad shut their bedroom door to talk. Still trapped in the arms of the tall, bald stranger, she was shoved into the van. She grew even more scared when she heard the van door slam shut.

She was in the van with the man. Alone. This was bad.

Momma and Dad had always told her to never get into a car with a stranger. She was going to get in so much trouble.

She felt a sting in her arm. It was the same kind of pinch from shots at the doctor's office. Sylvie started to cry into the fabric still being pressed to her mouth. She couldn't breathe and soon felt dizzy, like after she'd spun around too many times playing helicopter.

Momma! Dad! Help me!

Those were the words Sylvie's mind screamed, but the sounds coming from her mouth were nothing but moans.

Goldie still kicked and whimpered, but Sylvie could barely feel him as her eyelids grew heavy. Had he gotten wrapped up in the blanket too? Was that why he felt funny in her arms? She had to get home. Dad was going to be so mad. He'd never let her keep the puppy now.

The last thing Sylvie felt before her world turned black was the puppy licking the tears off her cheeks.

2

Rebecca West sat behind the desk in the back of the Shadow Island Sheriff's Department and tucked a loose strand of blond hair back into her ponytail. It wasn't her desk, and tomorrow she'd make that official.

The desk belonged to Sheriff Alden Wallace. He was only sixty-seven when he'd died on Tuesday.

Five days. Seems like a lifetime.

Although she didn't know the deputies of the small department well, Rebecca felt it was the least she could do to hold down the fort while the men and women of Shadow Island grieved the loss of their sheriff, who was more than just their boss. He was a father figure.

Such a tragic loss. More wasted life.

Everywhere I go, people die.

Guilt threatened to overtake Rebecca as the events of that fateful evening played on repeat in her mind. Wallace had signed off on the plan to lure the Yacht Club goons into a meeting. But it had been Rebecca's idea. And now the sheriff's body lay in state.

She touched the badge Wallace had given her. How had her vacation turned upside down so drastically? She'd come to the island to relax and clear her head. Instead...a good man was now dead.

Once the autopsy results had come in, Wallace's funeral was scheduled. It was this evening. Churchgoers could still attend Sunday services and, perhaps, lift an extra prayer or two to their deity on behalf of their sheriff of over forty years.

The front door opened and closed, pulling Rebecca from her depressing thoughts. Who could it be? She'd given the entire department the day off.

Deputy Hoyt Frost was a possibility. He'd talked his doctor into releasing him from medical restriction following an emergency appendectomy, but the man should've still been home healing. When a person had been murdered and time was of the essence, though, everyone on the force had dropped what they were doing. Rebecca respected Hoyt's dedication and had warmed to him throughout the course of the ordeal.

Deputy Darian Hudson should've been home on paternity leave. Like Hoyt, the young deputy had come in to help. Now, after such a tragic loss, holding his newborn might offer the glimpse of hope they all desperately needed.

As far as she knew, Deputy Trent Locke was still on desk duty after the shooting. She chose not to spare another thought for that man. Images of him racing down the dune that night sent a shudder through her.

That left the department with precious little in the way of personnel. Still, with everything else taken care of and her duties officially over, she could hand the reins back over tomorrow to the man who deserved to be holding them, which was Deputy Hoyt Frost.

It was a small island with little crime. He should be able to handle the job on his own while she went back to her original plans of relaxing and clearing her head.

While Hoyt wasn't in top shape yet, he could still stand in as acting sheriff until a special election was called. Or whatever it was they did here on Shadow Island. It wasn't Rebecca's problem anymore. Her case was closed.

She'd have to make herself available for the court proceedings, but that would be months away. Until then, she'd be a beach bum just as she'd wanted to be before Sheriff Wallace had come knocking on her door nine days before.

Nine days.

So much had happened during that short span of time.

"Morning, Rebecca."

Rebecca managed not to jump, but only barely. She'd been so lost in thought that she hadn't even heard Viviane Darby's footsteps approaching. Either that or the receptionist and part-time dispatcher was as stealthy as a cat.

Some detective I am.

"Morning, Viviane. I didn't expect to see you today." Rebecca tried to return Viviane's bright smile but failed, her lips threatening to tremble until she pressed them tightly together.

Misery was contagious because Viviane's cheerful expression melted off her lovely face, growing as somber as the black dress she wore. "To be honest, I couldn't bear to stay home. I need to stay busy until the funeral. Besides, I feel closer to Sheriff Wallace here..." Viviane glanced around the old sheriff's office.

Rebecca practically sprang to her feet and rushed around Wallace's oversized desk. It couldn't be easy for Viviane to see her sitting there. What had she been thinking? Today of all days.

"There's fresh coffee in the back. I made it from that new blend you ordered. It's good stuff." Rebecca held up her coffee mug as she attempted to change the subject. But the dread of telling her new friend that she was leaving her interim role as sheriff consumed her. She had to tell her new friend and didn't know how.

"Ohhh, I don't like that look." Viviane's dark eyes were filled with concern. "Are you leaving us?"

Among her many fine traits, Viviane was also intuitive. Rebecca was not surprised. Her heart contracted as she realized just how much she would miss hanging out with Viviane every day. Maybe they could still be friends.

The front door banged open, and boots clomped in double-time on the carpet, their thumping growing stronger with each step.

Rebecca and Viviane exchanged curious stares as Deputy Hoyt Frost charged down the hall, stopping in a huff at the doorway to the sheriff's office. Taller than her five-ten, he was so lean and wiry that she understood why the other deputies sometimes called him Scarecrow.

"We got a call about a missing little girl a few minutes ago." He wiped a sleeve over his forehead. "Her parents are going crazy looking for her. Trent's not answering his phone, and I'm going to need you to drive."

He spun on a heel and toppled sideways, shoulder hitting the wall. He winced before building up enough momentum to storm back the way he'd come.

"Dammit." The man might be back at work, but that didn't mean he was fully healed. Rebecca shook her head and handed her coffee mug to Viviane. She grabbed her keys. "Guess I'll see you in a little while."

"Good luck finding the girl."

This day wasn't going the way she'd thought it would.

She'd planned to cover the office so the others could attend the funeral. Then she was going to resign first thing Monday morning, return to her little beach house, sit on the patio, and relax with a good book until a few glasses of some alcoholic beverage knocked her out.

But how could she do anything close to that, knowing there was a lost little girl out there whose parents had to be going crazy looking for her?

Throwing open the door, Rebecca stepped out into the idyllic summer day and went searching for answers. To her left, she spotted Hoyt before he ducked around the corner of the building, most likely heading to where the department Explorers were parked.

"Wait up. Who's missing?"

Either Hoyt didn't hear her, or he was ignoring her, because he kept on going. For a brief moment, Rebecca debated walking away. She'd already done everything she'd said she would. In fact, she had done more. She'd gone above and beyond the call of duty for this island.

Rebecca had agreed to finish the one case involving another missing girl. Cassie Leigh. That case was closed. She'd even gotten a confession out of her killer and stopped him before he killed again. On top of that, she'd arrested two men on charges of transporting minors across state lines. Why shouldn't she be able to quit?

But Hoyt had said there was a missing little girl. Straightening the badge on her belt, Rebecca reluctantly chased after the deputy. By the time she rounded the corner, he was standing in the open passenger door of one of the Explorers.

"Let's go, Rebecca...um, West..." His face paled, and he swallowed hard. "Sheriff...Interim Sheriff...shit."

Compassion nearly swallowed Rebecca whole. It must be hard for him to know what to call her. His boss and very good friend had just died, after all. "Just call me Rebecca." She shook the keys. "Where are we going?"

He was already sliding gingerly into the passenger seat. "I'll tell you on the way. I can't drive. Doc's orders."

Moving on instinct, Rebecca slid behind the steering wheel. "Tell me what's going on."

"We just got a frantic call from a dad whose little girl has gone missing down at the beach. I'll give you directions as we go." He slapped the dashboard. "First things first, start the engine."

"Roger that."

Hoyt read from his notepad as Rebecca got the Explorer moving. "Sylvie Harper. Eight years old, long brown hair, brown eyes. Last seen wearing a pink swimsuit with ponies on it and carrying a box of colored chalk. Hair secured in a ponytail with a pink scrunchie. Been missing for more than an hour, they think. Last seen leaving a rental house a couple of blocks from Sand Dollar Beach to draw on the sidewalk with said chalk." He tucked the notepad into the breast pocket of his uniform. "Do you know what it means when kids go missing while wearing their swimsuits?"

Rebecca swallowed hard as she turned onto Main Street. She knew exactly what happened to little girls who went missing, wearing swimsuits or not. She wanted to keep him talking, though, and get a better understanding of his thought process. "Tell me."

Hoyt hit the siren. "It means they're probably heading to the water, or they're already in it. Her family's rental isn't far from the beach. She could easily have walked there on her own. They taught her the route home yesterday in case she ever got lost. And her dad said she's not a good swimmer."

Adrenaline raced through Rebecca's veins as she passed a slow-moving truck, ignoring the double yellow lines.

Hoyt braced his arm against the cruiser's jerky movements on the frame of the open window. "Shit."

Keeping her focus on the road, Rebecca studied the man beside her from the corner of her eye. His cursing surprised her, and so did the pained look that settled across his face.

"Are you sure the doc cleared you to come back to work?"

"He cleared me to come back to desk duty if I promised not to drive anywhere or lift any heavy objects. Pretty sure that means I shouldn't be trying to hold myself still while you're playing Earnhardt over there."

Hoyt had one hand on the dashboard and the other on the windowsill. Her driving wasn't *that* erratic. He needed to relax.

"If you can't drive, you can't run. What good are you back at work?"

"It's you and me or no one, West. Take the next left. Second right after that."

A memory from her past was triggered by the comment. A time when she'd been playing on the same beach and had gone in for a dip to cool off. The current had grabbed her and dragged her farther from land, no matter how hard she'd fought to get back. Her mother had had to swim out and save her.

"It's you and me, baby," Anna West had said. "I'll always save you."

She'd been Rebecca's hero that day, among many others.

Blood-coated linoleum.

Dried crimson flecks on the cupboard doors.

Slick floor under her feet.

Rebecca pushed away the memory of the last time she'd seen her mother and focused on not hitting any cars as she raced through the small island town.

Hoyt grunted beside her as she made the right-hand turn.

She needed to focus on the here and now. "What's the tide?"

He grunted again, this time without any sound of pain. "It's going out."

"Dammit."

If the tide was out, it would be easy for a little girl to be pulled out to sea if she was in the water already. When the locals talked about the riptide, they weren't joking. You couldn't see it. You couldn't fight it. You just had to try not to get sucked under until you broke free. Experts claimed the best thing to do was to swim parallel to the shore until you were free of the riptide. But little Sylvie wouldn't know that.

"Dammit times ten." Grabbing the radio, Hoyt called the station. "Viviane, can you rustle up Greg and ask him to grab a boat and head out to Sand Dollar Beach? Tell him what we're doing and that we have a missing little girl who can't swim."

"Right away. I'll tell him to hurry."

He set the radio back in its cradle. They rode in silence to the wail of the siren and the tires barking as Rebecca bobbed and weaved through traffic, drivers trying ineffectually to get out of their way.

Hoyt didn't need to tell her which house it was.

The siren caused heads to pop up like a field of prairie dogs after a predator had gotten bored and left. A small crowd of people stood outside what had to be the Harpers' rented beach house. Even more people hustled up and down the road, searching between houses.

It looked like the neighbors had already gotten in on the action. Which, to Rebecca, wasn't a bad thing, even if it was a bit of a surprise. "Is this normal?"

Hoyt flicked his eyes over at her and frowned.

"This. All these people." She gestured at the roving bands of people in the yards.

"A little girl is missing. Why wouldn't everyone be out and looking for her?" He turned slightly, moving stiffly, to face her. "I would hope this would be normal anywhere. If not…." He let the rest go unsaid.

She wouldn't disabuse him of his small-town view of neighbors helping neighbors. "Okay. I'll drop you here to meet the parents and then—"

"What are you talking about?" He pointed to a house with several people standing out front, huddling around a man frantically waving at them.

"Maybe you should get the details while I help with the search. You—"

Hoyt held up a hand. "You're the commanding officer, not me. I didn't sign any of that paperwork. You're in charge. I'm just along for the ride."

Before she had the car in park or uttered a word in response, the damn man got out and headed toward the gathering that was migrating toward them like herded cattle.

"What the hell?" Rebecca whispered under her breath.

This was a tiny tourist town with a small-town mentality. They didn't trust outsiders. They especially wouldn't trust one to lead them. But Hoyt, the most senior deputy on the force, had just told her she was in charge—after ordering her around this morning and complaining about her driving.

It was true, though. She had signed the paperwork. But only because she'd expected to work just the one case. Hell, she'd expected him to want to take over and see the last of her. Looked like she'd gotten caught in the red tape and would now have to work her way out of it.

Rebecca reached into the glove compartment and grabbed the digital camera stored there. Right where Wallace had left it. Maybe being in charge of the expensive tech was normal in a department this small. Or Hoyt was just trying to get away from her as soon as possible.

A shiver ran down her spine as she spotted the man who appeared to be Sylvie's heartsick father. And it hit her...today was Father's Day. Her stomach twisted, and she did something she rarely did. She prayed.

"Please, God, let this case have a happier ending than the last one."

3

Closing the driver's door, Rebecca snapped a few discrete shots of the people who'd turned out. She never knew what she might be walking into. Best to keep records of everyone. Not that she planned to mention to Hoyt, or anyone, how often perpetrators came back to insert themselves into the investigation and "help" with the search. That wouldn't do anything for morale.

But after Cassie Leigh, Rebecca knew not to trust any citizen of Shadow Island. This place had a darkness simmering just below the surface. She was learning there was no refuge from that gloom. But perhaps she could do her part to shine a light into those shadows.

Photos taken, she walked up to the group gathered in a loose horseshoe around Hoyt. People in uniforms tended to make folks feel better in times like this.

He jerked a thumb at her. "This is our interim sheriff, Sheriff West. She'll be leading the search and investigation. Sheriff, this is Joseph Harper, Sylvie's dad. He called it in. Mrs. Harper is off with one of the search parties." Hoyt's gaze turned intent. "Knowing the sheriff herself came down has given them a lot of hope." He indicated the entire group. "Of course, I already told them that our sheriff takes lost kids seriously around here."

How many times can he call me "sheriff" in one conversation?

Rebecca tried but didn't entirely succeed in stopping the flash of annoyance that crossed her features as she ignored Hoyt by turning her full attention to the distraught father. She clocked him at about six feet tall, with brown hair and brown eyes.

She wondered if his daughter took after him. She didn't have to wonder long, because he pointed his phone at her, showing a picture of a little girl who looked just like him, sitting on his shoulders with the ocean in the background.

"This is her. This is my daughter, Sylvie. Please help us find her." He stuffed the phone into her hands.

He was speaking of his daughter in the present tense, Rebecca noted, which was a good sign. Parents were always the first persons of interest in cases like this. But pleading in the present tense was an indication of innocence.

She took the device and studied the image more fully before meeting the father's terror-stricken gaze. She needed to calm him, help him think. "Of course, Mr. Harper, that's why we're here. But first, I need to ask you a few questions. Who was the last person to see Sylvie this morning?"

Rebecca noticed Hoyt was already taking notes, so she didn't bother to pull out her pad and kept her attention on the father.

The man looked ready to explode and deflate at the same time. Her question already had him bunching his hands in his hair as if he might rip it all out. "Me. It was me. As far as I can tell. I was making breakfast. She wanted to go outside and play. Found some colored chalk in the toy box."

Mr. Harper bent down and picked up the box of chalk at his feet, and he pointed to where it was obvious little Sylvie had been drawing. Something purple and round with different-colored lines smushed inside it.

She handed the phone back to him. "Go on."

"I told her she could use them so long as she stayed right in front of the house where I could see her. She's a good girl. We've never had a problem with her wandering off before. She always stays near the house."

"And what time was this?"

"Just before ten thirty, I think, or maybe just after. She was drawing me a cheeseburger." He took a shaky breath. "I've been on a kick recently singing 'Cheeseburger in Paradise,' but making up different words to it. It made her giggle."

This was a man who loved his daughter and spent a lot of time with her because only a loving, involved father could make out a cheeseburger in the scuffed multi-colored hieroglyphics on the concrete.

"So that's the same box Sylvie had?" Rebecca was afraid she already knew the answer.

"I came out to look for her after I didn't see her from the window. I found the box next to her drawing. I called for her, but she didn't answer. She always answers. She's a good kid."

Rebecca nodded. Of course, the father had picked up the box his daughter had left lying on the ground. It was the paternal thing to do, grab up the last thing your child had touched, as if it could connect you to them. He had no way of knowing it would also play havoc with an investigation.

"Does she have any friends nearby? Someone she met recently? Played with? Anyone at the beach she spoke to or interacted with?"

Mr. Harper shook his head through that whole line of questioning. "No one. We're not local. We don't know anyone. We're from Locust. Just wanted to spend a week at the beach. We came early to avoid the higher prices of midsummer." He waved a hand at the house. "We're not rich. This is the best I could afford. I just wanted to give my little girl a nice vacation. A good start to her summer. You know? She's a good kid."

The poor man nearly choked every time he spoke of his daughter in that way. As if being a "good kid" would protect her from the worst possible outcomes. That was something she'd heard before, in all kinds of cases.

We're good people.

She's a good person.

As if being "good" was a safety net. Sadly, the world didn't work that way.

If it did, I wouldn't be the acting sheriff right now. I'd still be back in the FBI, maybe even blessed enough to be vacationing with my parents like little Sylvie was.

"Does she have access to the internet? Could she have met someone online?"

Mr. Harper was already shaking his head again. "She's not allowed on the internet except to watch movies or do her schoolwork. She doesn't even have a phone. I didn't think she was old enough, and she doesn't care either."

It was clear the thought hadn't entered his mind, Rebecca realized. Someone on the internet communicating with his young daughter would breed horrific conclusions most people weren't prepared to consider.

"Sylvie would much rather be outside playing than using technology. We've been talking about getting her a dog, a lab or a retriever, so she can spend more time outside and go farther on her own. Dogs are good. A dog would have protected her. Or barked. Or something." He moved to the front porch, sat on a chair, set the chalk box at his feet, and dropped his head in his hands. "Why didn't I get her a dog? Or a phone?"

Rebecca followed him to the porch. She turned the other

chair to face him and sat as she swatted at a fly in front of him. "Sir, can we—"

"She could have called me. Oh, god, why didn't I get her a dog? She's a good girl and she really wanted one." Every sentence rushed out faster than the one before it. Complete panic was but seconds away. "Begged her mother and me."

Rebecca inched closer, worried that Mr. Harper might hyperventilate and be no help to them at all. "Okay, Mr. Harper, I need you to slow down. Take a deep breath. There you go. Slowly, in through your nose." She pushed to her feet. "How about we take this inside? Can you show me Sylvie's room?"

The distraught father looked at Rebecca like she was crazy. "She wasn't inside. She was outside. She disappeared from out here. I have to be here in case she comes back. In case she needs me."

Mr. Harper was gasping for air as if he'd just run a 5K in record time. And it probably felt like that. His mind was racing, and his body was trying to compensate.

Rebecca gave him a gentle smile, schooling each of her facial muscles to remain calm. "I understand. We have people searching for her right now, and if anyone sees her, they can tell her where you are. Or call for you. Only you can show us where your daughter was and help us gather the information we need." Rebecca took Mr. Harper's arm and gently helped him up before steering him inside the house.

What she didn't say was that parents were always the initial suspects in a child's disappearance, and Rebecca needed to get a better understanding of this family's dynamics right away.

"I'll wait right here." A tall brunette in florescent jogging clothes inched forward. "You go inside and help the police. I'll holler if I see anything."

Mr. Harper nodded and allowed himself to be led inside,

his breathing finally slowing down again. "Yeah. Okay. Thanks. Yeah."

It was a nice little house. A fairly common rental, everything quaint and clean, if a bit small and overly decorated with seashells and mermaids.

The kitchen and front room were joined into one big room. Each had exterior doors, one leading to the front yard and one to the back. Both doors stood wide open, as if waiting for a little girl to run in at any minute to pick up the bucket and scoop she'd left, slip into her pink flip-flops, and scram back out.

The windows were small but had gauzy, beach-themed curtains hanging in front of them. They afforded little privacy but were perfect for a photo shoot.

In the kitchen, a pan of cold eggs with one serving already plated was waiting to be eaten. A dirty bowl with the remnants of someone's cereal was in the sink, along with a glass.

"Who did you rent this from?" Rebecca asked.

Mr. Harper collapsed into the kitchen chair closest to the front door. "Uh, I'm not sure. My wife found it on a website. She handled all that, the booking and everything. I can call and ask her." He dug in his shorts pocket.

"Mr. Harper, would you mind if I take a look around the house?" Rebecca gestured down the hallway, the only place she couldn't see from where she stood.

He frowned, his eyebrows furrowing together. "But she's not in the house. She would have come out when we called if she were. She's a good girl."

"Unless she found a hidey spot and fell asleep and can't hear us," Hoyt said, entering the home. He scanned the room they were in. "Some of these old beach houses have hidden cubbies. Things you wouldn't notice normally, but to a curious kid, they become almost magical. Smugglers back in the day used them to hide bootleg rum. Homeowners now, especially ones that rent out, use them to store cleaning supplies or items like filters or mothballs. Stuff they don't want guests to have to worry about." He shrugged, as if it was the most common thing in the world.

Rebecca couldn't tell if he was making all that up on the spot, or if it could actually be true. Not in this house, though, since it was a newer model and not something that had been built and lived in during Prohibition.

Mr. Harper didn't seem to consider that, though, as he nodded along as if all made sense. That line seemed easier for him to swallow than the reality of the situation. That many kids who went missing were, in fact, just hiding in the house or nearby, either unaware or confused by the chaos their absence had caused.

"Oh, yeah, sure then. I haven't seen anything like that. Her room is the first on the left there. We stayed in the master, which is in the back. I can show you."

Rebecca waved him back into his seat. "Actually, Mr. Harper, why don't you go ahead and call your wife? See how far away she is. We need to speak to the owner too. I noticed there was a camera in the doorbell on my way in. If we can get the video, that could move matters along quicker."

They left him in the kitchen to call his wife and walked down the hall. The first door on the left turned out to be a linen closet. Still, they checked it. Hoyt reached up to the top shelf and pushed things around 'til he could see the very back.

Rebecca squatted to check the lower shelves to make sure there were no places for a small child to hide.

"Oh, hell."

Rebecca stood to see what Hoyt had found. He pulled down a brightly colored present. A child's writing scrawled across a blue envelope taped to the top.

To Daddy. Happy Daddy's Day! Love, Sylvie.

She blew out a long breath. "We've got to find her."

Hoyt nodded and placed the gift back on the shelf.

Finding nothing else, they moved on to Sylvie's room. Mr. Harper's voice reached them, and she listened as he talked to Mrs. Harper, asking where she was and how soon she would be back. Nothing suspicious caught her attention, so she headed inside the little girl's space.

A small open suitcase lay across one side of the queen-sized bed. It was full of tiny shorts and t-shirts and at least two swimsuits, both with horse graphics on them. Under the bed was nothing but a line of dust bunnies the cleaner had missed.

She and Hoyt worked naturally together, following the same pattern of him checking high while she checked low. He wasn't that much taller than her, but she didn't want him to try and bend over. As hard as it was on her knees, it would've been worse on his incision. She still didn't know how bad his surgery had been or how well he was healed.

They searched the bathroom the same way, and the master bedroom. Something they hadn't mentioned to the father, but went without saying, was that they were also looking for signs of violence or intruders. And hidden cameras.

Rental homes were good places to shop for victims, since families didn't know what should be there and what shouldn't, making it easy to slip in nanny cams or something more sinister. It was becoming a serious problem for law enforcement with the rise of rental homes. Owners setting up cameras to spy on unsuspecting guests.

They found nothing.

Every closet, suitcase, bag, dresser, and cupboard contained no hidden hatches and were free from any gadget that shouldn't be there. When they got back out to where Mr.

Harper was waiting, they searched the kitchen and front room the same way. He stood and followed them around, clearly needing something to do.

"I didn't think to look under the sink. There's a shed out back. Do you think she could be hiding back there? It's locked. I don't have the key."

Rebecca glanced out the back door. "I'll check it out. Were you able to get in contact with your wife?"

"She's just around the corner. When...when I told her Sylvie was missing, she didn't even get angry at me. Just got out of bed and started looking. Looked in the house, looked outside, started calling for her. Then, when we still couldn't find her, she went to look for where she might have wandered off to and told me to call 911. She was at the beach just now. That's why it's taking her so long. She didn't want to stop looking, but I told her you guys needed to talk to her." His eyes jumped to the front door again.

"Wives can get upset," Rebecca prodded, watching his expression and body language carefully. "It happens. Does she often get upset? At you or Sylvie?"

"What? No, no." He scrubbed his palms against the hem of his shorts. "She's more laid back than me. I could have driven down and picked her up. I should have picked her up."

"That's all right, Mr. Harper. We needed to check the house inside and out anyway," Hoyt reassured him as Rebecca stepped out the back door.

Just as Mr. Harper had said, there was a small shed there. It was a simple thing, four walls and a door with rusty hinges and an equally rusty latch held closed by a shiny padlock.

The rest of the yard was flat and sparsely covered in weeds and grass that blended into the neighboring yards on each side and behind. There was nothing else for anyone to hide in nearby, but she spotted other small buildings like this one in the adjacent yards. Those would have to be searched too. But for now, she tested the latch, then pushed along each wall of the shed. There were no loose boards, and the bottom was fastened securely. They would want to search it to be sure, but Rebecca couldn't see any way to climb inside.

It was a lot of ground to cover, and she only had a few deputies to help her do it. Was it going to be a race against the tide? Or a kidnapper?

4

"Did they find her yet?"

Rebecca turned as a woman, sweating and red-faced, came through the back door. *This must be the mother.*

"Not yet, honey, no. They need to talk to the owner. There's a camera in the doorbell. We need to get that for them."

"The doorbell?" The woman, about three inches shorter than Rebecca, was already flicking through the screen on her smartphone. She wore pajama shorts and a thin shirt, her hair loose and windblown. Her brown eyes were wide but focused. "I booked it through an agency. I didn't talk to the owner, but here's the email with all the contact information. I can forward it to you." She looked back and forth between Rebecca and Hoyt, then settled on Rebecca. "Or would you rather I write it down?"

Hoyt reached for her phone. "May I?"

"Of course." She didn't take her eyes off Rebecca as he took the device. "Joe said you searched the house? To see if she was hiding? We looked. I swear we did. That was the first thing I did."

Hoyt stepped outside, placing a call while reading the email. Before the door closed behind him, he caught Rebecca's eye, then pointed down.

"I'm certain you did, but it never hurts to check twice." Rebecca glanced at the door to see what the senior deputy was trying to point out.

"They were looking for hiding spots. Something I didn't think of, hun. Did you?"

Mrs. Harper shook her head. She turned back to Rebecca. "Oh, I'm sorry. I'm Heather, Sylvie's mom. We checked the house, then the yard. Then I thought maybe she'd gone to the beach, so I started walking. We were screaming so much, the neighbors all heard us and came out to help. They're still out there."

"Mrs. Harper, did you hurt yourself?"

"Hurt myself? What?" Mrs. Harper looked at her as if she were crazy. "No. I'm fine. It's my daughter. She's missing."

Rebecca stepped forward, pointing down. "You've tracked blood all over the floor."

"Blood?" She followed Rebecca's finger.

"You're bleeding. Your foot is bleeding. You should sit down."

Mr. Harper reached for his wife. "Honey, what happened?"

"What happened? I don't know. I didn't notice." She took his hand and let him lead her over to the table, where she took the chair he'd vacated. "I didn't think to put on my shoes. I ran down the street. I took the same path we took yesterday. The route Sylvie knew."

Mr. Harper lifted her bleeding foot.

Rebecca couldn't stop the hiss that was jerked out at the sight of it.

The foot was covered in road rash. A small line of blood was starting to form around the other foot on the floor too.

The mother had run the skin on the soles of her feet right off.

"Oh, honey, we should get this looked at."

Mrs. Harper waved Mr. Harper away, not even phased, as he wiped the bottom of her foot with his hand, then down his t-shirt.

Rebecca flinched. That was a bad idea. She could just imagine the dirt from his hands getting buried deeper into her open wounds.

Guilty parents wouldn't run their feet raw like that. Rebecca had met enough monsters to know that, but she wasn't ruling anyone out quite yet. Unfortunately, parents were statistically the culprits in situations like this.

"I made it to the beach and didn't see anything, but the guy next door said he found a purple chalk stick on the road near his house, in the direction she would have taken to get to the beach. I bet she's there somewhere. You have cops searching the beach?"

"Deputies should be there about now, yes. We're in the process of creating search radiuses and will be calling in backup to assist." The mother seemed like she would jump up and get on with her search any second now, so Rebecca kept talking as she moved away. "I saw a first aid kit in the bathroom. Let me grab that for you."

She was back in a few seconds, kit in hand. She handed it to Mr. Harper.

He took it with shaky fingers. "Thanks."

Pulling her phone from her pocket, Rebecca held the device up where they could see. "Mind if I record our conversation?" When they both agreed, she hit the app that would record all audio. After stating the date, time, and people present, she got down to business.

"Please tell me everything that happened this morning."

"I didn't wake up until Joe noticed Sylvie was missing. It's vacation, so I was catching up. He came and got me up after she didn't answer when he called for her. Maybe ten forty-five or so. This is so unlike her. Sylvie is always so well-behaved. I can't understand why she would leave the yard."

As the mother's tears began to fall, Rebecca turned her attention to the father, watching him as he did a shitty job of cleaning out the poor woman's wounds. "Okay, Mr. Harper, can you take me through, step by step, everything that happened this morning? Don't leave anything out."

Having something to focus on, some way to help his family, would help Mr. Harper to steady himself. He gave Rebecca a play by play. Finding his daughter waiting when he arose at nine thirty, wearing her swimsuit and with her hair pulled back in a ponytail, eager to go to the beach.

How he'd started breakfast while singing. How Sylvie had waited impatiently until she'd asked to go outside to play. How he'd agreed, if she stayed on the sidewalk, in front of the kitchen window. How he'd watched her continuously while she was drawing. And how, after he stepped away to get the juice out of the fridge, she was gone. That's when he went outside to look, scanning up and down the street, before coming back to wake his wife to help.

Mrs. Harper joined in, adding little pieces of information here and there. It read like every parent's worst nightmare. They'd done everything right. And, somehow, their only child had still gone missing in the blink of an eye.

"Is there any toy Sylvie might have taken with her if she was going to the beach? Or a towel? Anything she wouldn't have gone without? A favorite toy or doll?"

"Her flip-flops." Mrs. Harper's face fell as she stared over to the open front door where the small shoes sat. "She has soft feet like me. She wouldn't go anywhere without her flip-flops. The sand burns her feet." The last sentence came out as a wail. "She wouldn't have gone to the beach without her flip-flops!"

Mr. Harper hugged his wife as she broke down.

She grabbed his shirt, staring into his face as if searching for answers. "Oh god, she wouldn't have gone to the beach without her flip-flops! Where could she have gone?"

"Like you said, she's like you. You ran down there without your shoes."

"Because I was looking for her!"

"Maybe she was looking for something important too. Like you were." Now that his wife was breaking down, Mr. Harper became like a rock, steadying her. He held her face between his palms. "She's so like you. I bet she got excited about something. Or maybe she saw a bird and thought it was hurt and ran off to help it. You know how much she loves animals. She'd stop at nothing to help anything with fur or feathers."

Rebecca watched as the couple stabilized each other.

A knock on the doorframe broke up the tense moment.

Hoyt ushered an older woman inside. Rebecca frowned. While she was certain she'd never met the woman before, she did look familiar. It was something about her dark eyes and flawless brown skin. And Hoyt was smiling at her as if he knew her. He wouldn't have let just anyone in the house either.

"What have we here?" the woman asked Mrs. Harper with a knowing smile. "Looks like you've gone and hurt yourself. Ah, but there's a first aid kit, so we'll get you taken care of right quick. Up on the countertop, so we can have better access to the sink. There ya go now."

Looking a little stunned at the sudden intrusion, Mrs. Harper followed the directions and, with her husband's help, slid onto the counter.

"Sheriff, hun, go ahead and get me a bowl and some paper

towels." The woman gave orders as smoothly as a school-teacher, then bizarrely pulled a packet of sterile gloves out of the giant purse she'd set on the table and snapped them in place with the ease of long practice.

Rebecca looked at Hoyt for an explanation.

"Uh, Sheriff, this is Margaret Darby, our unofficial advocate. She's offered to come down and sit with Mr. and Mrs. Harper while the search continues."

As soon as he said her name, Rebecca noticed the resemblance to Viviane. She had her mother's eyes and smooth complexion. Except these eyes were now directed at her and not-so-silently telling her to get a move on. Rebecca turned and fetched a bowl for Mrs. Darby.

"Oh, right, right. Sorry about that. I was gonna introduce myself, but then I noticed all the blood and got distracted. You all can call me Meg. Now let me see those feet of yours. Don't worry, I've got first aid certifications enough to stand in as a school nurse. And I know road blisters when I see them. This is what happens when you run on these hot roads without any shoes on."

Mr. Harper jumped to his wife's defense. "She was looking for our daughter."

Meg took no offense at that. In fact, her brilliant smile only grew wider. "Well, of course, she was. She's a good momma. I'd have done the same thing in her shoes. Or not in her shoes, as the case may be. Have before too. Chased after my kids down the street without a thought for myself." She chuckled and patted the top of Mrs. Harper's foot. "So let's get you cleaned up and bandaged, so you can get back to it as quick as possible. We want you ready for when it comes time to pick your girl up, yeah?"

Rebecca handed her the bowl and paper towels and got a toothy smile in response.

"Thank you. Now, you go ahead and go on with your job.

Don't mind me here." True to her word, Meg started cleaning up the foot with the most damage.

"Sheriff, a word?" Hoyt still stood at the door.

Rebecca walked out the front door and down the steps, dodging the bloody footprints as she exited. Meg's voice floated out to them. "So tell me about this little girl of yours. She's eight?"

"Advocate?" Rebecca kept her voice low so the Harpers wouldn't overhear.

Hoyt gave a twitch of his shoulder that might have been a shrug. "Closest thing we have, locally. And she's trained for it. I think she might be trained for everything if it comes right down to it. She's worked here longer than I have. She can handle it. And we need everyone we can get."

"Were you able to get ahold of the rental agency?"

"Yup, and they sent over the video right away. Didn't even fight me on it after they made sure who I was. Nice folks there." He held up his phone where a full-color video was paused. "Looks like it happened just the way they said it did."

Together, they watched Sylvie walk out the door, her back to the camera, and lay down on the sidewalk in her swimsuit. She drew on the sidewalk for a short while. Then something off-camera seemed to catch her attention. Her hands flew up to her face, as if she was excited. Standing, she walked off and out of the range of the camera, holding two pieces of chalk.

Hoyt held up an evidence bag. "I collected this a few houses down."

It was a piece of purple chalk.

"Did anyone else touch it?"

Hoyt rolled his eyes. "Of course, they did. The man who found it and handed it to me." He nodded before she could even say anything. "I got a full print from him, Stewart Whiley, for exclusion."

"From that video, it does look like she just wandered off on her own. Her dad said she's an animal lover and might have run off if she saw an animal in need. A bird or something."

Hoyt looked grim. "Or she was lured off."

As much as Rebecca hated to think that way, a kidnapping was just as likely as anything else. "Let's continue under the premise that she's been kidnapped but hope she's just lost."

Hoyt cracked a smile. "You got it, Boss."

"Don't." Rebecca covered her eyes with her hand. The idea of her being anyone's boss was just too weird to even think about right now. "Just don't. You're old enough to be my dad."

He flinched as if he'd been struck. "A teenage dad, maybe. Respect your elders, young 'un."

Rebecca ignored the crack, and the less-than-ideal nickname, and continued as if he hadn't said anything. "Do you know anyone with access to a drone? It would help with the visual search."

"I do. I'll give them a call." He pressed his lips together. "Wallace and I discussed getting a drone for the office, but…"

"Might be a good place to spend some money." She pulled out her phone and started texting. "I'm going to have Viviane start working on an Amber Alert and notifying CART."

She'd worked with the Child Abduction Response Team several times over the years, and the skills they brought to the table during missing children cases were invaluable.

Hoyt raised an eyebrow. "Think CART might be jumping the gun a bit?"

Rebecca was surprised at his response and paused with her thumb over the send button. "The parents will stay on our radar, but I don't think it's them. This was smooth." She pinched her chin, thinking it through. "Too smooth. Too slick. If it was an abduction, it went off nearly flawless. No one saw or heard anything?"

Frost's sad headshake said it all. "Nope. Nothing."

"Then, no. I don't think I'm overreacting. Do you?"

He stared at the piece of chalk in the baggie. "No, it's the right thing to do. If she ran off to help a stray animal, she'd have dropped the chalk here where she was drawing, not down there."

"And her family seems loving and supportive." Rebecca sent the message to Viviane and began a second one. "Maybe they've got some skeletons in the closet, but nothing I've seen leads me to believe she ran away from home on purpose."

Hoyt blew out a long breath. "Especially not barefoot and wearing nothing but her swimsuit."

"Right." Rebecca began typing again. "I'm also asking Viviane to get someone down to monitor the docks. If this is a kidnapping situation, they could have Sylvie in a boat already."

The deputy frowned. "Who're we gonna get to do that?"

It was a good question. They had so very few resources.

"I'll have her contact the dock managers and see if we can get them on board to help keep an eye open for anything suspicious. I'll have her get in touch with the Coast Guard, too, to see if they can offer assistance checking boats and dragging the shallows." She sent the text without reading it over. Viviane was smart as hell and could fill in any missing blanks.

"What about private docks?"

Another good question.

She shook her head. "We can't cover everything, so we have to focus on the highest priorities first. As more resources arrive, we can spread out." She began texting again. "I'll see if Viviane can pull up a list of homes with private docks. We'll have the list ready to distribute if it comes to that."

There was still a crowd of people, half of them searching as the other half fixated on Hoyt and her. "Let's keep moving forward with the search. Get a recent picture from the parents so we can set up the Amber Alert."

"You got it. There're reflective vests in the trunk of all the vehicles, by the way," Hoyt said.

"Perfect. Put one on and stay here organizing the search. There are some buildings that still need to be checked. And we need to get a key from the agency to check the storage unit out back."

"I'm on it, Boss. And tell Viviane to start grabbing any video footage from nearby. She knows who has what and where." Hoyt moved off to do as she'd directed, already dialing his phone again to call the rental agency.

"And stop calling me *Boss*!" she hissed after him.

"Sure thing, Boss!"

5

R ebecca walked through the front door of the sheriff's office, still irked at being the person in charge.

"Hey, Sheriff." Viviane beamed at her with those sparkling dark eyes.

"Viviane?" Rebecca scolded, making her new friend giggle.

"I've already sent requests into CART and to the Amber Alert system, like you asked. And I called all the docks and the lifeguard station and asked them to keep their eyes open. Anything else you want me to do?"

"You can start by never calling me *sheriff* again." Rebecca smirked at her friend. "I don't even know how to do half the things you do. How can I possibly be the sheriff?"

Viviane shook her head in amused denial. "Well, I can't call you Interim Sheriff. That's too much of a mouthful. Plus, the list of things you're probably good at far outweighs what I do behind this desk. To be honest, I play a lot of games on my phone." She gave a very theatrical wince, holding her hands in front of her face. "Please don't fire me, Interim Sheriff."

Rebecca rolled her eyes. "How about just calling me Rebecca?"

With a dramatic flair, Viviane pressed the button to unlock the half door and waved her boss into the bullpen. "To make up for it, *Sheriff*...I'll bring you some beer tonight after we get off. How about that?"

Rebecca's mood darkened, and she glanced around just to make sure there wasn't anyone else in the building. "This is starting to look more like a child abduction. I'm not sure when, or if, I'll be leaving the office today."

"All hands on deck, then?" Worry chased the amusement away from Viviane's face.

"All hands on deck. Can you call everyone in?"

"Sure can. Darian did say to give him a call if things got too hairy, but I'm betting he just wants to get out of diaper-changing duty." Viviane frowned and gave an awkward shrug. "Don't forget, the funeral is this evening. Wallace's brother is on his way."

Rebecca dropped her face in her hands and gave it a good scrub. "This makes everything so much worse."

"Don't you have something for me?" Viviane held out a hand.

Rebecca set the bagged piece of purple chalk in it. "Not much of a clue."

"Sylvie was holding two pieces of chalk in the video footage. Maybe the second will lead us to some answers."

Rebecca headed toward the sheriff's office.

"His passwords are written on a notepad in the left-hand drawer." Viviane's instructions chased Rebecca down the hallway. "That's the small round key on the ring you have."

Every time Rebecca stepped into Wallace's office, she felt like a creep or a trespasser. The chair was an old-fashioned wooden swivel one, with a slatted back and what looked like a homemade cushion on the seat. Finding the key Viviane had described, she unlocked the drawer and saw the notepad was the only thing inside. She leaned over the desk and logged in, using the sheriff's credentials. Which, technically, were hers now.

She already knew how to use the database, so it was quick work to pull up a history of missing persons reports for minors. Ignoring the report for Cassie Leigh, the next most recent one was five years ago. A sixteen-year-old girl had snuck off from her parents' home. She'd driven to the mainland to go to a club. She was "found" when she drove back just before dawn and was caught trying to sneak into the house. No harm done there.

The case before that was much more tragic. A seven-year-old boy went missing from a local family's backyard. His body was found washed up on the beach three days later. He was wearing swim trunks and his new snorkel. All evidence indicated that he'd ventured out into the ocean by himself, and the tide took him, just as Hoyt had warned her could happen.

There was a notification that Rebecca's open case had been updated. Clicking over, she saw that Hoyt had added a picture of Sylvie Harper. It had been taken within the last two days. She was slightly sunburned, grinning up at the camera while standing on the beach, wearing a pink swimsuit sporting ponies. It wasn't one of the swimsuits Rebecca had found in the girl's room, so it was most likely the one Sylvie was currently wearing.

Now that she had the photo, Rebecca quickly made up the missing person flyer from the template.

Once that was printing, she pushed the marked button on the phone that would buzz Viviane at the front desk.

"Yes, Sheriff?"

Rebecca ignored the name. "Can we coordinate a DUI checkpoint on the bridge?"

"A DUI?"

"Yeah, set it up to look like a DUI stop, so we can check every car that tries to leave the island. How do you guys do that here?"

"Oh, that's smart. Yeah, I can set that up with the staties. They love doing those and will coordinate with other counties to assist. They get so much money from the tickets."

Rebecca exhaled a relieved breath. "Ask them to bring a sniffer dog too. We'll need to have the dog key on a worn article of Sylvie's clothes, so it can alert to her scent if it's present on a vehicle or person."

"Oh…" Viviane's voice went up a few octaves. "I see what you're doing. If a police dog alerts us to a vehicle, that gives us cause to search it."

Rebecca smiled. "Bingo. Can you send Deputy Locke over to get an article of Sylvie's clothes? He'll need a picture too. Hoyt just posted one to the case file. And what's the status on getting Coast Guard assistance?"

"They're sending help. Until they can get here, I called Greg Abner and asked him to head over with boats and nets."

They're all working like a well-oiled machine. She's even called in the retired deputy to lend a hand. Everyone knows their job and does it well. Except me.

"Thanks. Let me know when Greg gets out there, would ya?"

"Yeah, Boss."

Oh, yeah. Viviane had been talking with Hoyt, all right. Probably over the radio, which Rebecca still didn't have a handheld for since Wallace's had been damaged in the shooting.

There were a lot of things she didn't have yet. No uniform, no hat, no cuffs, no belt. Just her own gun and holster and the badge that still said *Deputy*. There was a lot of stuff she needed to get together, if she was going to work this job. Some of it could probably be found in this office if she wanted to start searching.

Rebecca eyed the well-worn wooden chair beside her. Realizing there was no way in hell she'd ever be comfortable sitting there, she hooked her fingers between the slats and dragged it to the other side of the room, setting it in the corner where no one else would use it either. Picking up the cheap and uncomfortable folding chair, she maneuvered it in place and finally sat down at the keyboard.

She was still searching the National Crime Information Center after filing her report when the sound of heavy boots clomping down the hall made her look up.

Deputy Trent Locke froze in the doorway, his beefy form taking up most of the space. The glare on his face could have peeled paint, but she didn't take it personally. He slapped a hand on the door, just under the nameplate. "Couldn't even wait for his funeral." Keeping angry eyes locked on her, he slid Sheriff Alden Wallace's name tag out of the brass holder. He squeezed his hand so tight around the black plastic rectangle, she wondered if he might break it.

As he turned to storm off again, his eyes fell on the sheriff's chair in its place of honor in the corner of the room. He paused for the briefest moment, then stomped off like a toddler throwing a tantrum, shaking his head.

Rebecca went back to work. The man was making his displeasure with her well-known. As if she didn't already know. That wasn't something she planned to deal with now, or ever, if she could help it.

As she searched surrounding towns using the NCIC, she found more cases like the one she was working. And they all had the same M.O. Amber Alerts had been issued on two young girls, one in Sandbridge and the other in Lynnhaven. Both children seemed to have walked away from their families, not to be seen again.

Both within the last week.

Could they be connected? If so, three cases made it more than a coincidence.

Rolling her shoulders to loosen the tight muscles, Rebecca did the one thing she hadn't thought she'd ever do again. Dialing from memory, she called the FBI.

6

Hoyt Frost watched as the newest volunteers walked off, heading to search the next section of the neighborhood. The man and woman had their heads down, hovering over phones displaying the island's evacuation map. It was public information and was already color-coordinated with enough detail for anyone to use. They tilted the phone to the side, stopped, and tilted it to the other.

Well, most people who understand how a rotating screen works can use it.

"Hey!" he yelled, catching their attention. He pointed to his left. "North is that way. You want to go south. The next road on your right."

The woman waved while the man went back to staring at the map before walking off again.

They had slowly been expanding the search area as each section was cleared. And still, there was no sign of little Sylvie Harper. Half the people had been sent to the beach, while the other half were walking down roads and through backyards.

It might have been overkill to send so many people to the

water, but it was damn easy to miss a small child in the waves, so he wanted as many eyes there as possible. They also had to search every dune, every rock outcropping, and every public restroom. And all with the hope that she was merely lost and not taken by some scumbag.

"Frost, we're here." Greg Abner's voice came through the radio set on his shoulder.

"See anything yet?" Hoyt tilted his head to speak into the mic. "I'm stuck down here on Bower Street keeping an eye out."

"We kept our eyes peeled as we headed over. Nothing yet, but we'll sweep the shallows."

Hoyt grimaced at that. Dredging rarely turned up anything useful. The riptide was too fast to leave anything close to shore for long.

"I've got Tim and Jack down here too. Saul's still heading over from the other side. He's going to check the current on his way." There was a brief patch of silence. "Is it true? Did West order all this? Does she think she's in charge?"

Hoyt laughed before he clicked his mic on again. "You and I both know that Viviane has always been the one in charge around here. She calls the shots, and you'd better move fast. Meg trained her, after all."

"That's a fact. And not one I would ever dispute over the radio when she can hear me. But you and I both know I was talking about Rebecca West. Is she really in charge? Not sure how I feel about that. Wallace's not even in the ground yet."

Hoyt didn't like where this conversation was going and wanted it to end before Greg said something stupid, like how he should take over. "Legally speaking, yes. Rationally speaking, she's the only person for this right now. It's not me, Greg. Never has been."

"I'm not buying it."

Hoyt glanced around to see if anyone was near enough to

hear. He didn't want this information to get back to the Harper family. "Switching to channel three."

It was the least-trafficked channel the station used. He didn't want this conversation picked up by every Tom, Dick, or Harry on the island. He wasn't worried about Rebecca West. She didn't have radio access yet.

"I'm here."

Hoyt picked up where he'd left off. "This goes no further than the two of us. I'm not back at a hundred percent. I had to get Angie to drive me to work this morning. Hell, I had to get West to drive me to the scene. I really shouldn't have been driving the day everything went down with Owen Miller and Stacy. Doc chewed me out for that. Said I could have wrecked and killed someone. Can't say he was wrong about that either. If I hadn't been so riled up, I wouldn't have done it at all."

There was a long break while Greg absorbed that information. "If you're that bad off, why the hell aren't you at home in bed?"

"Because bed is boring since the only thing I can do in it is sleep. Don't tell Angie I said that." He paused to let Greg have a chuckle. "Plus, you all need me. And to be clear, even if I was right as rain, West would still be better suited for this. She's got way more training than I do and way more experience with these types of cases than all of us put together."

"Even after she insisted on that meetup that ended in a shootout?" The doubt was clear in Greg's voice, but it didn't sound like he had made his mind up about her yet either. "She got Wallace killed."

Hoyt watched a car pull up to the house where the Harpers were staying. He'd been waiting on the rental agent to show up with the key to the shed. A tall woman in a business suit got out of the car, spotted him, and paused.

He waved at her to wait and started walking back there to meet up. "It might seem that way on the surface, but we all know the risks. Not the first time there've been shots fired. And she was down there in the sand too. And, let's be fair, we weren't there. We don't know everything that happened."

Saying that out loud made Hoyt think about just how true it was. Everything had happened so fast and so recently, and he'd been so hands-off with it all that he hadn't even bothered to read the reports on what had really gone down on the beach.

Truthfully, he didn't want to. He didn't want to read the firsthand action report of the last night of his friend's life. He didn't want to know if it was an ambush, a mistake, or just plain bad luck that'd changed everything.

Darian had told him what happened, but that was secondhand information from what Trent had told Darian, and it lacked some of the details. And the devil was in those details.

Could he have been wrong to trust in West? There was something about her FBI past too. Something Wallace had mentioned, but he didn't know the specifics of that either. There was a lot he didn't know, but he planned on fixing that as soon as he could. It was time to rip off the bandage to see what lay underneath.

"Well, why didn't she take more backup then? Didn't she get kicked out of D.C. for being a renegade and trying to take matters into her own hands?" Greg sounded indignant, and Hoyt understood why. Alden Wallace had been more than just the sheriff. He'd been a friend to them both. A damn good friend. And a hell of a boss and cop. But they had to face facts.

"I just know what little info Wallace told me about her and what I read on the internet. West might fly by the seat of her pants, but that doesn't mean calling in more backup was her call to make. Wallace was the sheriff and the officer in charge of the case. It was his person of interest that gave them the information about the Yacht Club wanting to meet up to pick up Cassie." Hoyt spoke softly, his emotions all over the place as he remembered Wallace telling him that West was going to get him killed.

Was it possible that Wallace knew more about what could happen that night than he'd told anyone? The sheriff had always been the man in charge of any cases that might be connected to the Yacht Club. And almost all of them had turned out to be nothing before. How could this one have been so very different?

He and Greg both knew whose fault that was. Whose call it had been to go down to that meeting with only three officers. Wallace had made that decision. And they all knew that guns had never been a part of the Yacht Club's history. There was nothing to make them think such a simple meeting would turn deadly. It had taken everyone by surprise. But one person had kept their head through the whole debacle and done everything to bring justice back to their island.

Rebecca West.

Greg coughed into the line. "It might have been his person of interest, but she was supposed to have his back and didn't. That's what got him killed."

"Listen, Greg. I—"

"You guys know I can hear you, right? I mean, this is the police band. The entire world can probably hear you."

Son. Of. A. Bitch.

When did she get a freaking radio? And, worse, how much of their conversation had she just heard? They'd been talking long enough that Hoyt had already made it to the woman waiting on him. He wished he hadn't made that crack about his wife and the bedroom now. Embarrassment ran up his cheeks and down his neck. If Angie ever heard what he'd said…

"Dammit to hell," Hoyt whispered under his breath.

The woman in the business suit shot him a startled look. "Excuse me? Are you Deputy Frost? I was asked to bring this key down."

"Yes, ma'am." He accepted the key. "Thank you for this. We'll call when we can return it. Thank you, ma'am. Sorry about that." He was babbling, and he turned away quickly, walking toward the shed in the backyard, where no one else could overhear him or see his red face.

Best defense is a good offense.

He clicked his mic back on. "Well, I guess you now officially know you're doing a good job, Sheriff." Hoyt wasn't prone to offering a compliment without an accompanying ribbing. "But hey, kiddo, congrats on figuring out the radio. I thought we'd never get you off your phone. Kids these days, Greg, am I right?"

Greg didn't respond. He was either laughing his ass off or just as embarrassed at being caught gossiping like a couple of old ladies at a church social.

West didn't join in with the joking. She kept it professional. Like he should have done.

"Update on the Harper case. There have been two similar abductions within fifty miles in the last week. I think we might be looking at professionals, so keep an eye out for anyone transporting. That might also mean that Sylvie's appearance has already been altered. Most common tactic is to cut or dye the hair and change clothes. Even if you see a young boy, still check it. NCIC and CART have been contacted and updated. FBI has also been contacted. They'll be sending someone."

"See, you're proving my point." He unlocked the padlock and opened the shed's door. Pulling out his flashlight, he stepped inside. "You should lead this case, as you're better than either of us working with the FBI. Those guys are assholes."

"You do remember I was one of those assholes, right?" West's voice was flat as a sheet of paper.

Never one to trust an expressionless tone from a woman, Hoyt opted to keep his mouth shut. The awkward pause felt like it lasted an hour as he checked every nook and cranny of the small space.

Nothing.

Hoyt broke the silence first. "In more recent news, the shed behind the house is clear. No one here and no sign anyone has been here or tried to get in."

"There goes that last hope. Okay. I'm on my way down to pick you up. We have some things to do."

"Copy that."

"Abner?"

It took a second for Greg to respond. "West?"

"Keep an eye out for any boats that could have unseen passengers."

"That would be all of them." Greg's voice betrayed his confusion.

"Exactly. You never know what might be hidden inside a boat. If anything goes sideways or just feels off, leave off. It's Wahoo season, so use that as an excuse to check all fishing vessels. We cannot afford gunfire with a child involved. Make sure you've got plenty of backup out there too. And Viviane called the Coast Guard earlier. They should be ready to lend a hand too."

Hoyt winced. So she *had* heard them talking about the shootout on the beach.

"Yes, ma'am. Didn't peg you as a 'hoo angler."

"Anyone who doesn't know when the Wahoos are running needs to move to Ohio. And might I suggest that if you two want to share gossip like old *men* at a church social, you use your phones to do so. We need to keep this frequency open for actual police work. There's a little girl out there waiting for us to find her. There might be three."

Thoroughly chastised, Hoyt rubbed his burning cheek and nodded.

She scoffed. "I can't hear you nodding over the radio, Deputy."

West's voice had a definite bite to it now, and for a moment, he didn't understand the implication of her words.

"Why don't you get in the car? We've got things to do."

Spinning around, he saw the cruiser parked in the driveway.

West was sitting behind the wheel, the radio mic in her hand, staring right at him. He'd seen that look on his wife's face enough times to know he wasn't going to enjoy this car ride.

You really messed up this time, you old fool.

7

I knew I shouldn't have, but I peeked through the blinds again, just in case.

Everything outside looked the same as it had fifteen minutes ago. Or was it five minutes ago? A driveway that was more weeds than gravel. The lawn was overgrown with sand burrs sticking up above dead grasses. And not a car in sight.

Just the way I liked it, and just the way I'd planned. Another perfect job.

I turned away from the window, wiping the trace of dust and grime from the blinds on my pants. It was important to keep up appearances. And this house had to have the appearance of being ramshackle and run-down from years of neglect. So much so that no one would ever think to enter it.

It had taken me years to perfect my methods, but now this house was the best hidey-hole I had. The deed was stuck in the courts over a contested will, because of some rich assholes who had nothing better to do than throw their money away on lawyers. With the fake bank notice in the window, decoy cameras at the front and back doors, and *No*

Trespassing signs all around, it wasn't easy pickings for the local teens or randy couples to try and squat in.

In truth, there hadn't even been movement on the deed situation in years, so there was no clear owner. I had just as much right to use it as anyone else. Hell, I was probably the only one who still paid attention to the damn shithole.

Over the years, I'd been forced to make a few repairs on the down-low. Fixing a leak in the roof, sealing a window after a storm, all things that would keep the house from actually falling down around me, or worse, damaging the goods I kept stored here between runs. I had my own little warehouse of sorts, and no one knew it even existed. And they never would.

They were all fools. And I was the shark that preyed upon the fools.

Beach towns like this one were full of prey. Middle-class bumpkins looking for a good time, with no connection to the community to raise any kind of ruckus, and no plans of returning. So long as I dressed appropriately for the season, no one ever looked at me twice. Just another damn tourist traveling through, and one that none of the locals would ever remember. I was in and out and on to my next drop-off or pickup. Cars, drugs, electronics, guns, girls...kids. Whatever was selling was what I was moving. And I was always moving.

There was never any telling what I would be transporting from day to day, which was why this place was such a treasure. Having a place to duck down, swap out, change looks. And all without cameras or witnesses.

My phone buzzed in my pocket. Right on time, which was always a pleasant surprise, despite the bitch I'd have to engage with on the other end.

"Will you be packed and ready to move when the time

comes?" Every word from the woman on the line dripped with aggressive distrust.

"Don't get on my ass, woman. Of course, I'll be ready. Hell, I'm pretty much ready now." I wanted to tear into her but knew that was just what she wanted. She always wanted to fight, and I was beyond sick and tired of it. If she wasn't so good at what she did, I wouldn't put up with her crap.

She grunted.

I grinned, knowing I'd won this round by not giving in to her jibes. It had taken me years to get used to her barbs and constant criticisms, but after so long, they just rolled off my back.

"The handoff is going to happen soon enough. Make sure the package is tied up securely. We want to make sure the gift wrapping looks good. They're paying us top dollar for this load."

"'Cause we deserve top dollar. We got them just what they wanted, right down to the sweet little smile and love of ponies. I really did a good job picking this one out."

I knew I'd messed up as soon as I said it.

"*You* picked her out?" She snorted and started in with her usual rant. "*I* picked her out. I was the one who saw her playing on the beach. You were too busy eye-fucking that blond skank tanning to even remember the job we were supposed to be doing. You were just tagging along while I did all the real work to earn this money. I was the one who got close and found out where she was staying and listened to her stupid stories about wanting a puppy."

Unbelievable.

I couldn't hold it in. "Are you fucking stupid or what? No shit, she wanted a puppy. What kid doesn't want a puppy? That's why it's such an old trick. It's probably the oldest trick in the book. That or free candy. Don't go trying to take credit for it."

"But I was the one who thought to use it!"

It was time to change the subject and get back to what really mattered. "Whatever. Did you get us the full amount we were asking for?"

"Of course, I did. I'm not about to let this go cheap."

Music began playing in the background. A bar. She was at a fucking bar. Again. Out spending money as soon as the job was on the books. Counting her eggs before they hatched and blowing our take before we were even paid. Just another reason why she was always coming to me to help her get out of a tight spot. Because I knew how to handle my finances.

"Good. With this last payment, I can afford to get that house in Mexico."

She snorted again, this time following it up with that sweet tinkling laugh of hers that had fooled so many men in the past. I had been one of them. Now, I knew better.

"You take your dumb ass down to Mexico after this, then. I'll see you back here in a year, broke and alone, begging for work after you've lost everything and can't pay off the whores down there. I'm going to stay right here, working with McGuire and living the life you promised me." Her voice turned nasty, and I knew she was just ramping herself up to tear me down. "Maybe if you beg, like when you convinced me to marry you, I might even allow you to work for me. You could be my piece-of-shit errand boy."

And there it was. The only time I'd really been a fool.

My damn optimism had made me do whatever she wanted in order to have a legal claim to the child we'd conceived. All because I'd wanted a son of my own. One I could do all the fatherly things with that I never got to do with my own dad.

She'd agreed, and for nine damn months, I'd done everything she'd asked of me. And then, she'd presented me with a daughter.

What the hell was I supposed to do with a girl? It had all gone downhill from there. Weeks of constant diaper changes, figuring out formula, buying clothes, and the nonstop crying.

"And look how well that turned out for me."

Silence.

I grinned and put every bit of mirth into my voice that I could. "The only good thing that came out of that was the primo price we got for her from your buyer. Still, barely enough to make up for the money we lost out on while you were pregnant. That isn't a mistake I'll be making again anytime soon. I can find someone else to bear me the son I deserve. They're much cheaper south of the border."

I didn't even wait for her response before hanging up. I knew she was just going to yell and curse at me. That was how most conversations with her ended. Unless we were actively working.

Just a little bit longer. Then you can get the rest of your money and go. And never have to hear her awful voice again.

Now that I was off the phone, the sound of crying caught my attention. I'd been hearing it for awhile, but I thought it was the gulls outside or something. But now it was getting loud.

It was coming from one of the bedrooms I'd set up with a special lock. This one could only be opened with a key. It didn't even have a handle, just the deadbolt I'd installed. It was harder to rattle a door if it didn't have a doorknob.

I'd soundproofed the room and knew no one outside of the structure could hear anything. Inside, though, the damn crack under the door still allowed the high-pitched cries that little girls made to slip through and travel to my ears.

The crying was grating on my nerves. I couldn't risk using more drugs on them again so soon, though. I didn't get paid for dead merchandise. My customers might be sick freaks, but so far, none of them were sick enough to want something like that. Though if they asked for it, I'd get it done.

I stomped over to the door, making sure they could hear me inside their little padded room. "Shut up, you stupid bitches! No one wants to hear your crying!"

"I want my momma! Momma!"

When I kicked the door, I heard a thud. Just like I'd thought. The little shit had been leaning against it crying, which was why I could hear her. I needed to re-insulate it soon.

When I'd put the merch in the room, I'd made sure to leave plenty of water and a bucket for them to use. There was no reason to risk opening the door. They could go a few days without food, and they were more willing to go to their new lives if they thought it would come with a meal.

"Your mommy doesn't want you anymore. That's why you're here with me. You did what you were always told not to do. Didn't you? You got in a stranger's van for a puppy. Why would your mommy want such a stupid girl?"

I kicked the door again, angry that they could be so whiny about such a little thing like being locked in a room for a few hours. These kids didn't even know what real suffering was.

"Now quit your crying before I give you a real reason to cry!"

8

Rebecca didn't even glance Hoyt's way as he folded into the cruiser next to her. As soon as he was seated, she backed out of the driveway and took off. Taking the turns that would lead her to the bridge connecting them to the mainland was simple enough. She could do it by memory, even though she wasn't familiar with this area. Having the ocean on each side made finding north and south child's play.

She could see him open and close his mouth several times out of her periphery, but she didn't turn her head.

Silence is often the best interrogation tactic.

Ever since she was a child, she'd always had a hard time keeping her emotions hidden. Everything she felt showed instantly on her face. It had been her Achilles' heel in training and later, while working for the FBI. But she'd found work-arounds.

Hoyt fiddled with his seat belt, trousers, buttons, and everything else he could reach. His discomfort amused her.

But remembering the conversation she'd heard over the open radio made it easy to keep the smirk off her face.

Where every law enforcement officer could hear. Where Viviane heard. Where anyone with a radio and a pulse could hear.

Viviane listened to the radio nonstop to keep up with what was going on. It was always running in a headpiece she wore that was usually hidden by her hair. Which meant she'd heard the men gossiping. And there was no telling if this was the first time either. What else could they have been saying behind her back? Viviane had never mentioned anything, but would she?

It wasn't like Rebecca even wanted to be in charge, nor did she care what Hoyt and Greg or any of the others thought about her. She did, however, care what Viviane thought of her. In the last few days, she and Viviane had become close. They might even be friends already. And Rebecca hadn't had a real friend in many years.

Traveling around the country made it hard to make friends or keep most friendships going. And losing herself to unraveling the conspiracy that had led to the deaths of her parents had finished destroying what few friendships had remained.

But she would do it all over again, even knowing what she knew now. Still, she missed having friends.

Viviane had loved Sheriff Wallace like family. Rebecca didn't want the woman to think she was the one responsible for Wallace's death. If these two jokers screwed that up, she was going to—

"So, uh, where we heading? Boss?" Hoyt cracked a weak grin, which she didn't return, making his wilt and slide off his face. He kept trying. "West? Rebecca? Sheriff?"

She attempted to unclench her jaw as she breathed slowly in through her nose and counted to ten before exhaling. She ignored his question and took the turn that would lead them to the bridge. That should be answer enough. Plus, they needed to focus on this case, and she wanted to make sure the DUI checkpoint was properly set up.

"Can you at least tell me what you're thinking, Boss?"

"One is a case. Two is a coincidence. Three is a pattern."

"Did they teach you that in the FBI?" Hoyt's tone was teasing.

She didn't tease back. "Yup, that's what the *assholes* taught me. So far, two Amber Alerts have been issued within the past week for two little girls from nearby towns. That gives us a total of three missing girls about Sylvie's age, but with different looks. If they were similar, this could be something like a serial kidnapper or someone trying to make a new family with girls that look like them."

"You think they're just gathering up any young girls they can find?"

"When they pick children that look vastly different, especially when they're girls, it's more likely a trafficking ring. Not to say that boys don't get picked up for that too. But girls sell for more. Generally speaking, girls are picked up in bundles, and boys are picked up and handed off one at a time. My gut tells me someone is stealing young girls to be part of a shipment that will be sold later."

"Jesus Christ." Hoyt looked a little green. At least he was no longer trying to make her smile.

"The first girl went missing five days ago from Lynnhaven. I'm waiting on a call from the detective in Sandbridge assigned to the second case. That one is just two days old. Once Sylvie went missing this morning, and I uploaded the details, all the cases got linked. So we're pooling resources and information." She motioned to the folder on the console between them without taking her eyes off the road.

Hoyt picked it up and took a slow, deep breath as he opened it. There were pictures of three little girls in there.

One blond. Two brunettes, but one with much darker hair. One brunette had long, straight locks while the other's shorter strands curled around her head. They looked nothing alike.

"I've heard about these cases, but I thought they were just basic. Kids running off. They both seemed too far away to involve us or be linked."

"As quickly as they were all taken, I'm betting they haven't been handed over yet. Gotta hope for the best and prepare for the worst."

"So you're going to treat this like a trafficking case? Not a regular kidnapping? Or even a missing persons?" He flipped to the next page. "Doesn't that seem like a bit of an overreaction? Maybe you should dial it back until we know more about what's happening."

Seriously?

"What's the issue, Deputy? Don't we have three families with missing daughters? I'm treating it like the case should be treated. The FBI doesn't only hyperfocus on big-city solutions. Children go missing every day. This is an appropriate response. Get on board or go back home and rest your belly."

"Wallace always hated calling in help from the mainland. They're dicks."

Rebecca glanced at him this time. "If it's an overreaction, there's no harm done. We're covering all the bases. The search is still going on. Deputy Abner's out dragging the shallows and checking boats. Deputy Locke is checking local businesses and residences for CCTV, asking for any additional footage that might have been captured."

"That's true."

Damn straight it is.

"Even if it started as a lost girl, she's been gone long enough that anything could be happening. Wouldn't be the first time someone took advantage of a lost child situation."

Her heart squeezed, and she fought a rush of tears that threatened to blur her vision. "And I don't need to remind you what happens, or could be happening, to those little girls at this exact moment."

"No, you don't. I can't let my brain go there." He cleared his throat. "About Trent. I—"

She held up a hand. "I don't care about Deputy Locke. I really don't. He doesn't know me. I don't know him. I'm more than happy keeping it that way."

She had no desire to stay on with the department. If she did, she might try to change people's minds about her. Other people. Not Trent freaking Locke. She gave zero shits about what a man like him thought of her. This wasn't about any specific male coworkers, though. Her lip curled up again at the memory.

"I worked a case, one of my first. Fourteen-year-old boy was missing. We were called in. I wasn't the agent in charge, of course. I was a rookie, just past my first year on the job. I was there to hump equipment and work the lines. There was a possibility it was a ransom kidnapping. By the time we'd compiled all the evidence...a missing bag, things he'd said to his friends, all that, it was clear he'd simply run away from home."

Rebecca took a sharp turn and cut off a box truck. She mentally smiled as Hoyt white-knuckled the chicken handle.

"We even knew where he was heading after we got into his social media. It was something he'd been planning for awhile. As soon as we knew all that, everyone was less eager to put in the legwork. We sent a beat cop to the friend's house, his destination, then we just waited it out. His body was found the next day."

She had to stop and take a deep breath. The lead agent had stayed with the parents while Rebecca was sent out to identify the body. It was one of the worst crime scenes she'd ever been called to.

Hoyt stared at her with wide eyes. "The hell? Was he in some kind of accident?"

Rebecca kept her eyes on the road. It was an awful memory and one that popped up in her head every time she had a case that dealt with children. It was also, unfortunately, a lesson in what to expect with cases involving missing kids.

Parents who were just waiting for the news their son had been picked up. A little worried but already planning to get therapy to help them all through it. They'd even made his favorite meal and were talking about other things too. How they'd punish him for the scare, but then take a family trip to get some time together and heal.

They'd thought the crisis was over. Everyone was ready to move on as soon as the boy returned. Until she'd had to make the call. Nothing had gone the way anyone had thought it would.

"An estranged uncle heard about him running away from home. The father's brother. They'd gotten into a fight over a pitiful inheritance years ago. Something about a treasured pocketknife of their grandfather's. They'd been out of touch for years, but he still talked with the rest of the family, so he heard about it. That's when he decided it was time to get his revenge on his brother. He was waiting at the bus stop, called the boy over, said he'd give him a ride. Then slit his throat and dumped the body in an alley."

"Over a pocketknife?" Hoyt was staring at her like he was waiting for her to confess she was lying. "Who would kill a kid over a pocketknife he didn't even have?"

"It wasn't about the pocketknife. It was about an old dispute that had festered for years. Spur of the moment, crime of passion and opportunity. Messy too. That's how most kidnappings are. Messy and opportunistic."

"This one's not messy…yet. Though opportunistic sounds about right."

"Which means?" Rebecca prompted.

Hoyt stared at the folder holding the pictures of three innocent lives. "This isn't like most kidnappings."

"Correct. It's too clean. Too quick. Too organized. Her father was right there in the window. But someone knew how to lure her away from his watchful eye. Took advantage of that split second when he wasn't looking. Then she was gone with no trace. That's a professional." She took her eyes off the road long enough to glance at the folder. "If my theory is true, three times they've managed to lure girls away from their families. That means they're good at what they do. Which means we need to do better."

"Which also means they've done this a hundred times." Hoyt shifted in the passenger seat. "You sure you're not just overreacting, seeing conspiracies where there aren't any, because of what went down in D.C.?"

What the hell?

"Excuse me?"

He held up his hands in defense. "I'm just saying that dealing with something like that can leave you jumpy afterward."

She gripped the steering wheel tighter. "I'm not jumping at shadows. And I'm not burying my head in the sand, pretending that no 'big city crimes' can happen in a small town. Crime happens, Deputy Frost. If you want to stop it, you have to be prepared to face it head-on. Half measures won't get anything accomplished."

Seething, Rebecca pulled up to the Shadow Way Bridge and became even more pissed that a roadblock hadn't been set up yet.

I'll take care of that.

Throwing on the lights but not the siren, she pulled onto the shoulder.

Hoyt glanced around, clearly trying to figure out what she was doing. "Um...are you planning to toss me off the bridge?"

It was crystal clear to Rebecca at this point that using jokes to cover uncomfortable moments was Hoyt's go-to. But now that he'd planted the thought in her head, the idea wasn't half bad.

She showed him her teeth. "I have a better idea."

Rebecca reached down and pulled the lever to pop the trunk, then climbed out without another word. The deputy was left scrambling as he tried to keep up. He reached the open trunk just as she pulled out a stack of cones, his hand pressed against his side.

Damn, she'd forgotten about his stitches.

Hardening her heart, she slammed the trunk closed and held up a hand to stop traffic before walking into the lane. She couldn't think of a healing incision when a little girl's life was on the line. Besides, he was the one who'd convinced his doctor to let him return to work.

Be careful what you wish for.

"What are you doing?"

"Setting up a DUI checkpoint." Rebecca started setting up the cones to form a line while Hoyt watched in confusion. "Don't want to wait until reinforcements arrive."

He walked over to her, lowering his voice. "What reinforcements?"

"Viviane called up the State police and Coastal Ridge Police Department. They were more than happy to help out when they found out what was going on. And that we would be giving them all the tickets they write. State patrol will be here soon with a sniffer dog. Folks will assume it's for drugs and such, but Deputy Locke should be bringing an article of

Sylvie's clothes so the dog can use that as a reference when searching the vehicles."

Waving the next car forward, Rebecca nodded toward the flashing lights coming up behind Hoyt.

Two Coastal Ridge cruisers, running their lights without sirens, pulled up.

A brick-faced man with a buzz cut got out and approached with his hands on his utility belt. "I'm looking for Sheriff West. Captain asked me to bring you the Sandbridge kidnapping files. They're in the car."

"That's me. I'm going to need you to give me a ride back to the station, if you don't mind." She glanced at her slack-jawed deputy. "Frost, you've got this until the rest of the calvary show up. Cooler of waters and breath analyzer are in the trunk. Once I can, I'll get someone out here to pick you up. No driving."

She finally allowed herself a little smirk.

Hoyt stepped closer to her. "You called up the neighboring PD? And State? That's...not how we do things."

Seriously?

"Who's *we?*" She didn't even try to keep the bite out of her voice. "The Four Horsemen of Shadow Island? Stomach Surgery, Paternity Man, Asshole Locke, and the Old Guy?" She took a step closer and barely managed to not poke him in the chest. "Because we don't have the time or the personnel to not accept help. This isn't a local problem. Everyone else understands that, Frost. Time for you to start thinking about the bigger picture here."

She didn't wait for him to come up with a response. She started to head to the Coastal Ridge cruiser but paused. On second thought, she wasn't quite finished.

Rebecca turned and looked him dead in the eye. "Didn't you hear? There's a new sheriff in town."

9

"Thanks for the ride and for your help."

The officer, whose name she hadn't paid attention to, shot Rebecca a little salute before pulling away from the curb in front of the sheriff's department and heading back to the Shadow Way Bridge. He'd been playing courier for her, and then chauffeur, but his final role was as Hoyt's partner at the checkpoint.

Once Trent Locke had acquired an article of Sylvie's clothing, he and Hoyt could sit on the bridge and talk about Rebecca all they wanted. Not that she gave a damn.

Quit giving a damn!

The deputies talking about her behind her back was annoying, but their distorted view of who was at fault for Wallace's death was a serious issue. She knew the truth about what had gone down and didn't plan to stick around long enough for it to become a problem. It was the fact that they could smile at her face. Well, Hoyt could.

That was what had pissed her off. The logical part of her mind reminded her that Hoyt had been defending her, but the cynical part wondered what he'd said in private. As he'd pointed out, it was a band radio. He knew he could be overheard.

"Who was that?" Viviane leaned forward over the desk to peer out the window as Rebecca walked in.

"An officer from Coastal Ridge PD. He brought me the files from Sandbridge and was on his way here anyway, so I caught a ride."

Rebecca turned her focus to the files in her hands. While the digital versions had all the pertinent information needed to make a case, the copies of the originals had all the notes and speculations from the officers who were working on the case. Things that were too ephemeral to add to official reports.

Never one to discount a cop's gut, Rebecca had asked for everything to be included. There were copies of scraps of paper and notepads. Including the parts that she really needed, such as the girl's likes, interests, and hobbies.

She came to an abrupt halt as she bumped into the locked half door.

Viviane hadn't buzzed her in, but instead stared at her with an amused smile.

"What?"

"You didn't hear a word I said, didja, honey?"

"Uh…" Rebecca cast her mind back. "You asked who dropped me off. I answered."

Viviane nodded, her chest shaking as she held in a laugh. "And then I asked where Hoyt was. And the cruiser."

"Oh, I dropped him off at the bridge to search vehicles and left the cruiser with him. I'll send someone to pick him up later."

Viviane lifted an eyebrow. "Who you going to send?"

It was a good question.

"I hate to pull Deputy Hudson off his paternity leave, but we—"

Viviane lifted a hand. "I'll call him. He'll understand."

"Thanks."

Rebecca pulled her set of keys out and waved the fob at the door to unlock it. A magnetic fob was so much more sophisticated than what she had expected from a station as old as this one. The door unlocked silently, and she pushed her way through.

"By the way, you remember what I told you earlier, right? About what today is?"

"Sunday?" Rebecca furrowed her brows, scanning her memory. "Can we walk and talk? I need to update the file."

Viviane hopped up out of her chair, unplugging her headset with a practiced move and tucking the cord into her belt. "Well, yeah. It's Sunday, and Wallace's funeral is this evening. His brother is coming into town. And we've got no one to meet him and drive him to the funeral like we'd planned. He's expecting us."

Rebecca closed her eyes, forcing her mind from the files in her hand. "I forgot to tell you that I have that covered. The mayor is going to pick him up instead."

"The mayor?"

"Yeah. I called him earlier and explained the situation. He and his wife are going to pick up Tom Wallace and take him to freshen up after his trip, then bring him by to meet us and pick up Sheriff Wallace's personal effects."

"Oh." Viviane perked up, her face relaxing as her worries lifted. "Do you need any help with his belongings?"

Rebecca turned into the doorway of the sheriff's office and gestured to the small stack of boxes in the corner behind the chair. "I could use another set of eyes, that's for sure. I've not had much time to pack up Sheriff Wallace's things. Honestly, it just feels wrong for a stranger to be going through his stuff. Can you help with that?"

"Yeah, sure. Let's see, we need his mug, his pen stand,

his…." Viviane poked around the room, opening drawers and checking shelves. Running her fingers down the spines of a few books, she added them to an open box.

A sad, wistful smile reached her eyes as she continued to look through the books. Probably remembering fond times with the man she'd worked beside for so long.

Turning her attention away, Rebecca sat in the hard, molded, fiberglass-and-steel chair she'd been using and opened the NCIC database again, checking for any updates. There had been no other cases linked to this one. That could be a good or a bad thing. Fewer cases meant less information, but it also meant fewer victims. There were a few flagged as possibly connected, but they were years old. Rebecca pulled those up. Before she could read them, her phone rang.

"Shadow Island Sheriff's Department, Interim Sheriff West speaking. How can I help you?" She hated how smoothly that rolled off her tongue and winced as Viviane gave her a big grin.

"Um? Are you the sheriff?" A man's voice came over the phone. He sounded shaky and confused.

"Yes, sir. How can I help you?"

"I'm Sam Dixon from over in Sandbridge. My daughter, Chelsea, went missing two days ago. The detective told me you might have some information, but he didn't tell me what. He said I should call you. Have you found her?"

The hope in the man's broken voice tore at Rebecca's heart, and she sat a bit straighter. "No, sir. I'm so sorry, but no, nothing yet."

Viviane turned from the bookcase she was still searching through and bit her lip.

"Oh." He whispered the word.

Rebecca squeezed her eyes closed at the depth of helpless resignation that was conveyed with just that one word.

"I just hoped. You know."

"I know, sir, and I completely understand." Rebecca kept her tone professional when all she wanted to do was comfort the man. Comfort wasn't a luxury either of them could afford right now. "But I'm sorry to say I'm working a case very similar to yours."

"Yeah. No. That's...that's basically what the detective said. I should have known better. They've already talked to everyone in the hotel. And the next hotel over. They even brought in drones to check the nature preserve nearby. But so far, they haven't found anything. Not a single clue." Mr. Dixon's voice trailed off, and Rebecca could hear soft sobbing in the background. "We just hoped..." He gave a laugh that was so broken it cut right through her thick skin. "I never knew hope could be such a terrible thing."

Rebecca struggled to keep her tone even. "I understand that, sir. I know how painful it is to hope, but I do ask that you don't give up. Keep hoping."

Viviane pointed to the door and started leaning that way. As soon as Rebecca nodded, she turned and scampered away from the painful conversation.

"Now, I know you've been through this a thousand times already, but can you tell me what happened to your daughter? Both of you, if your wife is with you."

"Nothing. I don't know. We were at the beach. Doing the usual stuff. Swimming, reading, making sandcastles. It was hot. Of course, it was hot. It's the beach. But Chelsea wanted ice cream to cool down, you know?"

"I know, sir. What happened next?"

"I gave her money. A ten. And asked if she remembered where the ice cream stand was. It was one of those booths they have along the beachfront where everything costs extra. It was close. I thought it was safe. We both did. We were right there. She wouldn't be gone more than a few minutes." His voice cracked, and the crying in the background got louder.

Rebecca was a silent witness to their shared pain and grief.

"I'm sorry. It's just…she was gone before we even knew. After ten minutes, when she didn't come back, I walked up to see what was taking her so long. Thought maybe there was a big line, or she got distracted. There're so many shops with cool things in the windows to catch a kid's eye. And she was nowhere around. I looked all over. There are carnival games and arcades. She's not really into things like that, but I checked anyway. Maybe she got distracted or lost or something. You know? Kids get distracted so easily."

"Of course."

"And she's never really had the best sense of direction. But it was broad daylight and still on the same block. It was more than half an hour before we even thought to call the cops. By then, she was gone. Just gone."

That matched what was in the reports, all corroborated by witnesses and CCTV. Almost everything had been captured on camera. Except for the moment when Chelsea was taken. That camera, by the ice cream stand, had been broken, and no one had noticed until they'd checked the footage.

"Is there anything you can think of that seemed out of place that day? Parents often have a sense of things when it comes to their kids. Even if you don't know why, was there anything that caught your attention that just didn't feel—"

"A white van." Mr. Dixon nearly yelled the words. "One of those big box vans that are used for deliveries. An older Ford, I think. It had those big mirrors on the side like you get when you're hauling a trailer or something. But it wasn't hauling anything, didn't even have a hitch attached. But he had those big mirrors anyway."

"He?" Rebecca wrote down the description furiously, hoping she could read her own writing later.

"Yeah, a guy was driving it. Had a hat on, but I could still see him. He was just sitting there, like he was waiting for someone. Kept checking his mirrors."

Rebecca perked up. This wasn't nothing.

"Can you tell me what he looked like?"

"White guy, hadn't shaved, real tan, probably in his early or mid-forties. But he wasn't there when Chelsea went missing. He left before then."

A woman's voice cut in. She assumed it was the mother. "Well over an hour before she went missing."

"Are you Evelyn Dixon?

"Yes, I'm Chelsea's mother."

"Thank you, Mrs. Dixon. Do you remember how long the man remained in the area or anything else about him?"

"The van was gone before we had our snacks, which was around two. The man's hat was blue, with a white logo with a picture of some kind of bird in the middle. He wore a gold wedding ring."

Rebecca was impressed by the woman's memory. "You have amazing recall."

Mrs. Dixon snorted. "It's a blessing and a curse. Trust me, there are many things I wish I didn't remember."

Like the day her daughter was taken, Rebecca imagined.

"What else do you remember?"

"His hands were smooth, not calloused. I know it's normal to people watch when you're at the beach, but he was sitting in his van doing it, and I can remember wondering if he was waiting on someone. He kept tapping his ring finger on the outside of the driver's door, making a pinging sound. That's what made me notice him."

"Did you tell the detective about him?"

Mrs. Dixon cleared her throat. "No, we didn't think about him at the time. Like I said, he was gone well before Chelsea went missing. And he didn't seem to be watching us or anything. Or Chelsea or any other kids. Just looking around. Seemed a bit impatient. Like he didn't want to be there."

So he was suspicious enough that he had set off both their parental instincts even without interacting with their child. And the mom had even checked to see if he was watching other children in the area, not just hers.

"One last thing. Mrs. Dixon, can you tell me about your daughter?"

Sniffles were her only response for a few moments. "Well, she's nine but small for her age. She's got curly brown hair and—"

"No, I don't need her description. I have all of that. Can you tell me about your daughter's personality? You said she's bad with directions?"

"No, well, she's not bad at following directions." Mrs. Dixon's laugh was filled with sadness. "If you tell her how to get somewhere, she can usually find it. But like, she couldn't tell you if she was facing north or east. Or figure out where she is. That's why we only let her go someplace close by, like that ice cream stand. It was so close to where we were sitting. If I'd just turned around instead of watching the water, I could have seen her the whole time."

Before she could break down again, Rebecca asked more questions. "What else can you tell me about her? Does she like horses?"

"Not really. She likes cats, though. And ice cream. And books."

"She really likes books." Love permeated the mom's voice. "My girl is a little bookworm, but she still makes plenty of friends. She's got lots of friends. She's so sweet and kind-hearted that everyone just loves her."

The mother's voice was clearing up the more she spoke, so Rebecca helped her along. "She's an extroverted bookworm?"

She was rewarded with a small laugh.

"That she is! I know it's a bit of an odd thing, but she is. She likes to talk with people. Get to know them. I think she probably gets that from reading. I've heard that people who read a lot of fiction are more empathetic than people who don't read much."

Rebecca jotted down her own notes on the copies in the folder. "What's her favorite type of book?"

"Oh, just about anything. But lately, she's really been into things like *Howl's Moving Castle* and that *Young Wizards* series. Oh, and a book called *Given to Fly*. She was really excited about that one recently."

Rebecca would do a quick search later to see what kind of books they were. It seemed far-fetched, but clues sometimes came from the most random places.

"Was she acting any differently that day? Did she seem to be interested in anything specifically?"

"No, not really." The father answered this time. "She was a bit more tired than usual, but then, she'd been up all night, watching movies with us. It's vacation, and the hotel has all the movie channels. So we sat around and watched some we'd been meaning to. Those new superhero movies."

"She loves those too."

Rebecca sensed a theme here. "This is all very helpful information. Can I reach you at this number again if I have more questions?"

"Of course." He was so eager to offer. "Does this change anything?"

"It might. I need to check a few things. We do still have a missing child here, but if I have any more information, I'll call you back."

"We're staying at the Four Palms Hotel. Room 318. If you can't reach us on this number, you can always call the desk.

We're staying here until we get our daughter back." He sighed before adding, "No matter what you find."

"Right." Rebecca's heart squeezed. "Hopefully, we'll speak again tonight."

Rebecca ended the call, still jotting down notes and checking the files. There was something about that van that seemed familiar, but it wasn't in the reports.

A sharp rap on the door made her look up. Trent Locke was standing there, once again glowering at her. As if she cared.

He sneered. "Viviane said you needed to see me, *Rebecca*."

"Deputy Frost needs help with the DUI ruse we're using to check all the vehicles leaving the island. Can you drive out there and relieve him? He's supposed to be on light duty and bending into cars over and over again can't be good for him."

He snorted. "What? Like you suddenly care about the health and well-being of all your fellow boys in blue? I know you're just loving it, the wannabe girl cop who couldn't cut it in the FBI but thinks she still has what it takes to run things."

Rebecca gave him a flat stare. "I care about Deputy Frost making a full recovery as soon as possible. Because once he's recovered, I can turn the reins over to him. He's at least competent enough to follow standard operating procedures and doesn't try to play John Wayne."

She lifted one eyebrow as she looked him up and down, letting him know without a word that she found him lacking in every one of those aspects.

"Why you—"

Rebecca didn't let him finish. "Wallace told me Frost was the best officer he had and that he always had his back. Why do you think the sheriff asked me to step in and help with the Cassie Leigh case?" Rebecca stood and placed both fists on top of the desk. "Because he couldn't trust the staff he had on duty to get the job done."

A bead of sweat trickled down Trent's temple. "How dare—"

Rebecca barreled on. "If a man you worked with your entire career thought so little of you, what makes you think I give a single fuck what you think of me, *Trent*? Did you forget that I know exactly what happened that night and why there needs to be an interim sheriff?"

Trent turned beet red, and a vein under his eye started to throb. He approached the desk and leaned in, hunching his shoulders and clenching his fists.

For a couple of beats, Rebecca's heart rate sped up. Had she pushed him too far? Was he actually such a hothead he was going to throw a punch at her? That could be bad.

They were already running with a skeleton crew as it was. Trent had just gotten back from administrative duty. They couldn't afford for him to be suspended or wind up in the hospital if he took a swing at her. Part of her wished he would, though. Wallace had been a good man. He didn't deserve to go down the way he did.

She relaxed her fists, sat down, and turned her attention back to the important work on her desk. If she paid attention to Trent's whining, he'd just keep on throwing a tantrum. Ignoring him was the best option to get him to leave before he did something he would regret, and she would enjoy way too much.

"If you're going to relieve him, give him a call and let him know you're on your way. If not, I'll try to get Deputy Hudson out there to cover it once he's available. And they need an article of Sylvie's clothes too. Did you get that?"

After a heartbeat, he nodded. "Yeah."

"Good. The staties need that for the dog at the checkpoint." Rebecca leveled another glance at him. "We still need to find that kidnapped girl, and maybe the other two as well."

It wasn't a command. It wasn't even an order. It was a

choice he could make for himself. He could choose not to go, but he would look petty as hell if he did, knowing there was a hurting cop standing out there waiting for relief.

Honestly, Rebecca wasn't sure which way he'd go.

And she didn't care.

10

Hoyt waved the last car in the line on. He was thankful traffic had slowed down, but he knew it was just a lull. Soon, people would be leaving the beaches, and the cars would be stacking up again. He grabbed a bottle of water, grateful West had thought ahead far enough to stock a cooler before she'd picked him up.

His stomach was hurting something fierce now. The hole where the drainage port had been removed was still healing and ached almost all the time. He'd slapped a bandage on it before getting dressed this morning and was more than a bit concerned at the damp stickiness building up in it. He hoped like tarnation that it was just sweat.

Pacing a bit, he turned away from the other officers who'd arrived to work with him and casually glanced down. There was no wet mark on his shirt. He let out a relieved breath and took another sip of water.

His phone rang, and he was hoping it wasn't Greg taking West's advice to keep their conversation off the radio. It wasn't a number he recognized, but he answered anyway.

"Frost here."

"Sheriff Frost, this is Chief Baxter from Lynnhaven. I hear we've got cases that might be linked."

"Sorry, Chief, I'm not the sheriff. Deputy, like always. You might want to call the station to talk to Interim Sheriff West. She's in charge."

There was a loud and disgusted grunt before the man spoke again. "West? Isn't that the FBI woman who screwed up and got your sheriff gunned down? How could an FBI agent take over as sheriff? Heard she didn't even visit the man in the hospital."

Hoyt froze. "Who told you that?"

"One of my boys drove down to the hospital the night it happened. Talked with your guy, Trent, who told him what went down. Said she didn't even ride in with them."

Hoyt's bullshit meter was going off the chart. Not at what Chief Baxter was telling him. He believed everything the chief was saying. Hoyt was doubting everything he'd been told about that night. He needed to get his hands on the After Action Reports. And possibly the forensic reports too.

"Sir." It never hurt to give a bit of courtesy before telling someone they were completely wrong. "*Ex*-Special Agent West was a sworn deputy hired directly by Wallace at his insistence. She was maintaining the crime scene, securing the prisoner as well as dealing with the wounded and the dead. Once she was able, she came down to the hospital and sat with me until she had to get back to work as the only available officer on duty that night. The next morning, she solved the murder case we were investigating. Might I add, she saved another young woman from being murdered in broad daylight at the same time? She's earned my personal and professional respect, as well as the right to be Interim Sheriff. And I'll argue with anyone who says otherwise, sir."

As the words came out of his mouth, Hoyt realized just how much he meant them. When push came to shove, he had no doubts about West's abilities or her dedication to the job. Today would have proved it if she hadn't already.

This time the grunt had a ring of respect to it. "Well, that's a whole different kettle of fish, isn't it?"

"Yes, sir, it is."

"You need to put a lid on the rumor mill down there, Deputy. That kind of talk ends careers and eats at the trust of a department."

"Yes, sir, I will. As soon as I can."

"All right, then." Papers shifted on the other end of the line. "We got an official request this morning for our records, but it was from West, who I was told wasn't the sheriff, so I didn't fulfill it. I'll get the detective in charge of the case to get everything together and send it right over. Our dispatch knows your dispatch, so I'm sure he has the fax. We've already updated NCIC."

"And the FBI?"

"The Feebs are involved too? Well, of course they would be. Do you have an agent on scene yet?"

"Not as far as I know, sir. But you should really call Sheriff West," he stressed the word *sheriff*, "and get the update from her. She's running lead on this one. I'm just standing out here on a bridge, checking cars, sir."

"Well, if you're checking cars, let me give you the bare-bones breakdown before I send her everything we've got. Nine-year-old Emma Bright was abducted from a firepit at one of our local beach bars. The dad had too much to drink and was dozing off. He thought the mother was watching the girl. But mom was rocking out with the band and thought he was watching her. At least two hours passed before anyone knew Emma was gone. No witnesses, so no description of a perp. The girl is four-four, skinny at fifty-five pounds, and has shoulder-length blond hair with green eyes."

"Yes, sir. Sheriff West already gave me a picture of her.

I've got it right here in my SUV for reference, but I appreciate the update." He knew the grin on his face made it through to his tone, but he couldn't help himself. He had to show off that West had already outpaced the chief of police. His phone chirped that he had a text message. It'd have to wait.

Chief Baxter cleared his throat. He obviously didn't like being talked to like that. "Seems you were right about your interim sheriff. I'm glad I was wrong."

Hoyt's view of the man changed on a dime, and he almost regretted rubbing it in his face.

"I'll let you get back to it, Deputy. Let us know if you need any other help."

"Thank you, sir. I appreciate it."

The call ended, and Hoyt noticed a car turning from one of the side roads and onto the highway, heading for the bridge. It was one of their cruisers.

Speak of the devil, and she will come.

Watching the Explorer approach, he decided to get a little revenge for her crack earlier about nodding into the radio. He called West's number.

"West speaking."

"Hey, Boss, you going to be hanging out with us peons to check all these cars?"

There was a slight pause. "I'm a bit busy emailing the Coast Guard to get more boats in the water. Why? Do you need help?"

"Oh, I thought that was you driving up—"

"Could be Deputy Locke. I told him to let you know he was coming to relieve you." The disdain she managed to steep into her words was a thing of beauty. He thought only Southern women could manage such a feat. He wondered if she was going to bless his heart as well.

He checked his notification screen, remembering the text

he hadn't yet read. It was from Trent, letting him know he was on his way.

"Just now saw Trent's message."

"If it's Locke who just pulled up, have him take over for you. If it's Hudson, give me a call back so I can rearrange some things. I need to make some calls."

"Yeah, Boss. I'm on it. Trent's here. What do you want me to do now?"

"Sit tight."

"I can drive it—"

"No. Doctor's orders, remember?"

Hoyt's side twitched at the reminder.

He almost told her what the Lynnhaven chief had told him but decided to have a word with Trent first.

"Roger that." Disconnecting the call, he watched Trent pull his cruiser up behind the first one and climb out.

Hoyt scowled as he walked down to meet the younger man.

"Got an interesting call just a moment ago."

"From Rebecca, I take it?" Trent had a nasty sneer on his face that Hoyt was more than willing to wipe off for him.

"No, from the fucking chief of police over in Lynnhaven. Some idiot told his people that we had an FBI agent here pretending to be the sheriff, so he called me instead. Know anything about that?"

Trent stiffened before shaking his head. "I didn't say she was pretending to be the sheriff. I said she was acting like she's the sheriff."

"She *is* the fucking sheriff until a special election is held to vote in a new one. And you know that!" Hoyt roared, not caring who overheard him now. "I don't give a flying Baby Jesus if you like it or not. If it hurts your ego or what. We've got a job to do out here, and there can be only one person in charge. That's Interim Sheriff West. Got that?"

Trent swallowed hard and opened his mouth. His angry eyes told Hoyt he was about to say something else stupid.

He had no intention of letting him. "Furthermore, you're telling other officers she couldn't be bothered to show up to the hospital for Wallace? You know full well she was doing her job and keeping the crime scene intact, so Wallace's killers would go to jail for murdering a police officer and not skate on some technicality because the scene was compromised after you left it!"

"Frost, come on—"

"You went spreading rumors about her that night. About a fellow officer of the law, when you knew they were lies. That stained *our* reputation with the other agencies, and now it's making it harder to work with them. You couldn't have known we'd be part of an interagency search for trafficked kids today, but that's no excuse for being an asshole. You made us *all* look bad."

Trent's nostrils flared as he blew out air and looked away as if he were chewing over his words before speaking. "I didn't mean to make *us* look bad. I didn't think Wallace was going to die. Or that Rebecca would still be here. I was mad, and I was venting to a buddy from Lynnhaven, who came down to check up on our sheriff. I was there alone, and I thought Wallace deserved better than that. When a cop's down, every cop within fifty miles should be there, giving blood and showing support. Rebecca West wasn't."

Shaking his head, Hoyt rested his hands on his hips. "You acted like his friend, but—"

"He *was* my friend!"

"He was my friend too, dammit. And, shit, West liked him. Why else would she work for the man? She showed up later after handing over the scene and dealing with the prisoners. Once she was done with her duties as a cop. *Not before.* Because of that, the men who killed my friend will hopefully go to jail for the rest of their miserable lives. You would have known that if you hadn't left the hospital so early."

Trent opened his mouth, then shut it, then opened it again.

"Don't even fucking speak! Go do your job. And make sure no one sneaks any children past you. There are pictures in my car of the three girls we're looking for. They might be disguised, so keep your eyes sharp and make sure the staties get little Sylvie's clothes the second they arrive with the sniffer dog. We've got one approaching now."

Trent turned to look, then marched up the bottleneck to where he would stop the car.

And just like that, Hoyt felt the full weight of everything he had lost again. Grief pulled at him, making his shoulders sag, which pinched the stitches that still weren't fully healed. If he could get away in time with this investigation still ongoing, he had plans to see his friend tonight, which usually was a good thing. But tonight, it would be in a church, with Wallace laid out in a pine box.

The car that had been driving up the bridge stopped in front of him.

Sighing at having to explain what was happening to yet another person, Hoyt leaned over to talk through the open window. "Go ahead and drive up to that other officer. We're doing a full DUI stop."

"You're Deputy Frost, right?"

That got Hoyt's attention. He looked at the kid. He seemed familiar, but Hoyt didn't know his name. "I am, but Deputy Locke is conducting the stop now. So if you'll just drive up to him, he can get you through and on your way."

"I'm not going through. I'm here for you." He gave a little half smile that wilted quickly as the deputy scowled at him.

"Why?" Hoyt rested his palm on the windowsill and took a better look at the driver. He was a young man, probably still in high school. He had on black trousers and a black shirt with purple down the side and a local printshop name tag still pinned on. "What do you need, son?"

"You. I mean, this is weird, but the sheriff called my manager and asked me to pick you up. I was going to make a delivery to the station on my way home, anyway, so I said no problem." He gulped, his eyes going wide. "At least she said she was the sheriff. Did I do something wrong? Am I being punked?"

"The sheriff called?" Hoyt's radio crackled.

"Frost, I've sent a civilian driver to get you. I need you here ASAP."

Well, I'll be damned.

"Roger, Sheriff. He just got here. Thanks for the ride." Not sure how he felt about this, Hoyt walked around the car to the passenger side.

Before getting in the vehicle, he took a few moments to calm himself, breathing deeply and trying not to think about anything. He hurt. He missed his friend. All he wanted to do right now was go home, call Wallace to come over for a few drinks, and tell him about the mess Trent had made for himself this time.

But he couldn't do that. He wouldn't do that ever again.

11

If I had to listen to those kids for much longer, I was going to go insane.

Their stupid cries were already grating on my last nerve. The first two had been properly cowed into quiet submission after just a couple of smacks. But that new girl must have been a bad influence, because now all three of them were crying loudly. Again. After I'd trained them so well. Even worse, they were yelling for food. As if the brat hadn't eaten just that morning at her yuppy parents' house.

Kids were so spoiled these days. They expected to eat every few hours.

I wasn't going to put up with that shit. Kids were to be seen, not heard, and would damn well do what they were told. I chucked my empty beer can in the garbage. Standing, I pulled my belt from my pants. I wrapped the tail around my hand just like Dad had taught me when I was younger than these whiny brats. The buckle jingled cheerily as I headed for the door to their room.

Another sound broke through my haze of anger and

stopped me in my tracks. Reaching into my pocket, I fished out my phone.

Seeing the number on the display did nothing to calm me. I could always trust my wife to ruin a good time.

"What do you want?"

"How big is that place you're getting in Mexico?"

The out-of-the-blue question confused me.

Why in the hell is she asking this now?

Having been burned once before, I knew the best way to treat Tammy was to give her as little information as possible.

"It's a three-bed place on two acres with a workshop. Why?"

"Three beds, huh? Maybe I'll come down and join you." Her voice was soft and sweet. The voice she used when she wanted me to agree with her.

"What happened to staying and raking in the money with the boss?"

"You're my husband, remember? What's yours is mine."

"And what's yours is mine," I responded, in the same mocking tone. Then it hit me. "Is that why you're not going to keep working for this new guy? Because anything you make will end up being half mine?"

She gave that light, tinkling laugh again, the one that always made me a little bit nervous. It was the one she used when she was working someone over.

"That might be it. But really, this place is getting boring, and I bet there's a lot more opportunities south of the border."

"You know what retirement means, right? That means no more jobs. No more looking over my shoulder. No more having to worry about ending up in jail again."

"Oh, you were never really in jail. They were just holding you 'til the court case was over. They found you innocent, so what's the big deal?"

Rage boiled up inside me, and the leather wrapped around my fist stretched across my knuckles as I clenched it. "It was the same fucking place! Just because I wasn't found guilty didn't keep me out of lockup while waiting on trial."

The same damn line, every time. And what the hell did she know about it? She never even visited when I was locked up. All the while, she managed to dodge any suspicion by piling it all on my head. Playing the poor, pitiful wife of the bad man she couldn't control.

Back then, she'd sworn it was to keep us safe, since the authorities couldn't fully pin anything on me and adding her into the mix would have given them more evidence.

"Maybe we'll just do one more job after this one. This was so easy, it would be a shame not to strike while the iron's hot. I'll set something up with my guy when I see him tonight. Remember to make sure the merchandise isn't *defective*. They're paying for purity, so don't go dirtying it up."

Dirtying it up? What the hell? I wasn't like those sick fucks on their fancy boats. I liked my women old enough to know what they were doing.

"I know how to do my job. The two others will be all healed up by the time they're picked up for delivery. I'm not screwing up my payday."

"Good, cause—"

"You just do your job, bitch. Get the second car prepped so we can move off this island and get ready for the pickup. I'm ready on my end."

I hung up on her and ground my teeth together. The crying hadn't stopped for the entire time I was on the phone. It was so distracting. Anytime I dealt with Tammy, I needed to be on my A game. But those little brats messed with my head the whole time.

Had she managed to get something past me? What was all that talk about the house in Mexico? And new opportunities?

I shut it all down, though. This was my last big haul, then I was out.

"I'm hungry! I want my momma! Somebody, please help me!" The whiny voice rang out.

I snapped around.

A shadow at the gap in the bottom of the door moved and caught my attention.

The stupid new girl had shoved her face down to the floor in order to scream at me. To scream at *me*!

Throwing the useless belt aside, I lunged at the door and kicked it as hard as I could, slamming the wood into her whiny little face. The scream that followed was music to my ears.

"Your mommy doesn't want you, girl. You left her for a fucking puppy! You're mine now, and you're going to do what I tell you. Now, shut the hell up, or I'm going to give you a real reason to scream."

After all, a few bumps and bruises above the hairline wouldn't drive down the price that much. I'd just take it out of Tammy's half. She was the one who'd picked this brat out of a sea of brats after all.

Can't leave any big marks? I knew plenty of ways to get around that and still teach them a lesson. There was a phone book around here somewhere.

Grinning, I searched for it.

12

The poor kid from the printshop looked like he was going to swallow his tongue the whole way back to the station. He also stayed three miles per hour under the speed limit. Which was easy to do when you stared at the speedometer every other second. He was probably a stoner. Those types never got comfortable around cops.

It was the longest trip back to the station Hoyt had ever taken. Thankfully, there was an open parking spot with plenty of room, so the boy didn't wet himself trying to parallel park.

"Thanks for the ride. Did you want me to take in whatever you're delivering?" Hoyt offered, thinking it was most likely a package that had been mailed to them.

"Ah, yeah. There're two boxes in the trunk, if you could." The kid hopped out of the car and walked around to the trunk, where Hoyt met him. There was a regular paperboard box and a much longer one that wasn't nearly as deep. "If you could grab that one. It's fragile, though. So be careful."

Leaning carefully into the trunk, Hoyt prepared himself for the pain as he lifted the large package. Surprisingly, it was lightweight. Probably not even more than he was supposed to lift, according to the doc. It felt like it was mostly bubble wrap from the squishy exterior. It certainly looked like it, though there was something darker in the center he couldn't make out.

"Well, let's get this inside. I'm sure you're ready to go home after working all day."

The kid pulled his work shirt off, straightened the white tee underneath it, and reached for the box. "Oh, I'm staying. I'm here to volunteer. So like I said, I was coming here anyway." He picked up the box and headed for the door.

It opened before he got there, and West leaned out. "Thought you might need a hand."

Holding the bubble-wrapped package up, Hoyt shook his head. "We got it all. What's so impor—" He stepped through the doorway, and a familiar movement caught his eye. "Angie? What are you doing here?"

Wearing a pretty floral dress that showed off her tanned arms, his wife stepped forward and gave him a kiss. "I brought you a change of clothes."

West took the package out of Hoyt's hands and walked past him, motioning for the kid to follow her. "Go get cleaned up. You've got fifteen minutes."

"But what's—"

Angie pushed a hanger with a garment bag at him and followed it up with a small leather satchel. "You heard her. Go get cleaned up." For the first time, Hoyt noticed his wife was wearing a dress. One she usually reserved for church or special occasions. He didn't have time to say anything about it as she continued to push him.

Hoyt checked his watch. The funeral wasn't for two more hours.

He took small steps as Angie pushed him toward the back of the station. "Uh, Boss, I got a call from the Lynnhaven

Chief. He got confused, which was why he called me. But he said he's going to send over everything he's got on their case now. You should get it soon."

West waved him off as if that mattered far less than whatever was in the paperboard box the kid had set down on the reception desk. "I already got all that. Don't worry."

"How'd you manage that?" He was forced to keep walking past the desk as his wife pushed him along. He didn't dare try to stop. It would have pissed Angie off. And he didn't want to piss off his wife.

"I had Viviane call Coastal Ridge and had them request it directly from the detective. Got them to make a copy and send it over with everything else. That's what I got from the cruiser that gave me a lift back. I've already read through it all, so don't worry about it. Go get cleaned up. We're running out of time. Chief Baxter was stonewalling me for some reason, and I'm entirely too busy to deal with dead ends."

Nodding and no longer having a reason to hold back, Hoyt gave in and walked to the locker room to get changed. He had no idea why his boss and wife were so insistent on him getting cleaned up, but they were serious about it. Angie had even packed his shaving kit.

What the hell is all this about?

A quick glance in the mirror showed Hoyt could use it. It wasn't much, but his five o'clock shadow had become more much noticeable once most of it was taken over by white and gray whiskers. Something he wasn't exactly thrilled about. He liked to think he wasn't vain, but he also wasn't as old as he felt right then. Looking in the mirror, he was afraid both of those things were wrong.

He chucked off his shirt, tossing it on the bench behind him, and opened his kit. Inside was his razor and gel, along with deodorant and a little baggie with a washcloth in it.

I guess she really meant it when she said I need to clean up.

He picked up the cloth and saw a glass bottle underneath it. His cologne. That he only wore on date nights or to special church events. Could Angie have conspired with West to get him to take her out tonight?

No. That was insane. They were in the middle of a case and had a funeral to attend. There was no way she would do something like that. Right? He'd never worked for a woman boss before and wasn't sure what to expect. Well, besides his wife. It had to be something else.

He reached over to open the garment bag and get what he assumed was a clean uniform. It wasn't. It was his dress blues. The ones he'd planned to wear to the funeral tonight.

Oh.

It was too early for the funeral, but maybe there was something planned before the service that he needed to attend. Then why wasn't Sheriff West in uniform?

You idiot, she doesn't have one yet.

For a moment, he almost reached over and locked the door. Just for a minute. Everything was getting away from him, and he needed a few moments alone. Deciding it was worth the risk, he flipped the lock.

Letting out a deep breath, he slowly lifted his undershirt. He had to back away from the mirror in order to see it. The stitches on his lower abdomen were bright pink. Not red like he had feared, and neither was the bandage. The one that he'd been worried about. With a gentle poke, he moved the latex-covered gauze. It didn't stick to anything, and he let out a breath of relief. He hadn't messed it up. So far.

Dropping his shirt back down, he turned on the hot water. On a normal day, it took him five minutes to shave and two to get dressed. But he followed his wife's guidance and gave himself a quick wipe down and felt nearly church proper by the time he tied his shoes.

He thought he heard a high-pitched engine whine for a

bit and reminded himself to check the A/C unit before he left for the night. *If* he left for the night.

Hoyt didn't want to miss his best friend's funeral, but he knew Wallace would understand if he had to. There was a job to get done, and Alden Wallace would have told him to go save those kids. There was no better way to honor the man than to do exactly that.

Unlocking the door, he walked out, ready to tell West he should get back to work instead of whatever she'd planned for him.

The steady hum of dozens of people's voices echoed down the hall.

Did they find Sylvie?

If they had, and God willing they had, then he could still go to his friend's funeral.

Moving as quickly as he could without running, Hoyt headed to the front. West was sitting in Viviane's seat, alone in the *Employees Only* area. Viviane was standing next to her mom and Greg in the lobby. Melody Jenkins, the late-night dispatch, was also there, standing next to Darian—also in his dress uniform—and his wife. The mayor was standing next to a man who looked suspiciously like Alden Wallace, right down to the gray beard and blue eyes. Seeing him, Hoyt's eyes went wide, and he slowed down as he tried to figure out what was happening.

Behind the assembled crew of the sheriff's department were a few other people from around town. People he'd known all his life, like the local Baptist preacher, and a few he barely recognized.

The printshop kid was pressed against the side wall, looking a lot less nervous now that he was standing with a few other kids his age. There were even a few men in uniform from Sandbridge, Lynnhaven, Coastal Ridge, and even Wilmington. An honor guard from the departments that had worked with the sheriff in the past.

Mayor Ken Doughtie took center stage, moving into the open area right before the half door. "Ah, Deputy Frost, I'd like to introduce you to Tom Wallace."

"We've met before, Mayor. It's been a few years now, but you haven't changed all that much." Tom reached his hand out to shake.

The shock of seeing so many people who had suddenly arrived had scrambled Hoyt's brain for a bit, and he hadn't immediately recognized Alden's younger brother. They'd only met a few times. Tom lived someplace out west now, he thought.

Tom gave his hand that extra squeeze and pat that Alden had so often used. "Hoyt, I know you're real busy around here, so I'll get right to it. Out of everyone living, you probably knew my brother the best."

Hoyt glanced over at Angie, who was beaming at him, tears swimming in her hazel eyes. *Is that pride in her eyes?* "I'd like to think so."

"Then you know my brother wouldn't want to risk anyone else's life just to stand around his grave and tell pretty lies. Especially not the lives of three young girls. I heard about what's been happening today. Damn shame."

"He was a cop's cop, blue all the way through," Hoyt agreed, not sure where this was going but feeling oddly hopeful. He glanced over at West, but she shook her head slightly and pointed to the mayor.

"So the only thing that makes sense is to postpone the funeral. Just a few days. Wallace would approve."

Postpone the funeral?

Relief washed through Hoyt, and his shoulders relaxed. As much as he wanted to see his friend one last time and have a chance to say goodbye, his duty required that he keep working. He'd never felt so conflicted before in his life, and having that resolved was a huge weight off his heart. "I was just thinking the same thing. He'd kick my rump if he caught me hanging around sipping punch when there's work to be done."

Tom smiled, though sadness softened its effect. "I bet he would. He could be hardheaded, that one. But a funeral isn't just for the fallen. It's also for those who loved him. So we're gathered here, right now, to take a few minutes to honor my brother, your friend," he held his hand out to Hoyt, then motioned behind him, "and our beloved sheriff by installing this commemorative photo where he can continue to watch over the community he loved so much."

Hoyt followed his gesture, and his breath caught in his throat. Alden Wallace smiled up at him from a glossy black frame nestled in a thick pad of bubble wrap. The package he'd brought in had been opened. A handful of wide, black elastic bands were piled beside it. The markers for their badges they would use to honor their fallen officer.

Reverently, he took one and noticed that Darian was already wearing his. Meg, Viviane, and Melody had larger bands on their right arms. He couldn't see if West was wearing one but assumed she was.

"Alden never had any kids of his own. That always bothered him. Until he made sheriff, then he had all of you to be his family. I think it's only right that it be you, his most trusted and loved deputy, who hangs his photo on the wall here."

Wiping a shaky hand over his mouth, Hoyt read the plaque.

He had to clear his throat before he could speak. "Serving with Integrity, Honor, and Commitment."

The warm, familiar arms of his wife wrapped around his shoulders, and he took a moment to lean into her embrace.

But everyone was watching, and waiting, so he kept it brief. Lifting the metal frame, he turned around. Someone had draped black crepe paper in a rectangle on the wall. There was a small table just below it that already had some of the flower arrangements and cards that had been delivered over the last few days.

Larry, the local handyman who took care of all the work in the building, stepped forward. He was wearing a collared shirt with khaki pants and holding a cordless drill. That was the sound Hoyt had heard while getting ready. The holes were predrilled, with anchors already set. All he had to do was hold the plaque where Larry directed as he secured it against the wall.

Once that was done, Hoyt found it hard to let go of the frame. For this tiny moment in time, he was able to say everything he had wished he had said while the man was alive, even if only in his mind.

Taking a deep breath, he stepped back and dropped his hands to his side. His right was immediately grasped by Angie. His elbow was wrapped in an embrace by Viviane, who gave him a sisterly hug. Wallace's "family" stood there for a moment of silence.

Hopefully, no one expected him to say anything profound because, right now, he couldn't think of a single thing.

"Preacher, if you'll lead us. I think we could all use a bit of prayer before we go back out there." Darian's voice cracked as he spoke.

"If you'll all bow your heads with me." Always a man of eloquence, the preacher asked for peace, protection for the protectors of His flock, and mercy for the lost lambs still waiting to be found. He closed with a simple thanks for everyone who was in attendance and to ask for guidance for those who came out tonight to volunteer. Everyone said, "Amen," and lifted their heads again.

Opening his eyes, Hoyt marveled at how much had been put together on such short notice and took a thankful and much-needed shaky breath.

Turning around, he reached out and took Mayor Ken's hand. "Thank you, sir, for putting all this together. This is precisely what Alden would have wanted."

The mayor smiled. "I'm glad to hear that, Deputy Frost. I hoped I was doing the right thing. But I have to admit, this isn't my doing. I was just the chauffeur for this one. Interim Sheriff West set this all up. Even got the picture made and framed. Called everyone and got schedules lined up. Not sure how she finagled the Coast Guard to come in like she did, but she did it so the others could get here."

For the first time, Hoyt realized that the whole crew wasn't there. Trent was still out running the stop. Could she not get him in? That didn't seem right. Surely, if Coastal Ridge had enough guys to send as an honor guard, they could have sent some to cover his lane. So why hadn't she?

He looked over to where West sat, still wearing the same clothes she had been, answering the phones so everyone else could have this bit of time together. She'd gone out of her way, during a crisis, to make this happen so the department could come together to grieve while she covered for everyone.

West caught him looking and raised one eyebrow.

He glanced around then at everyone else in uniform, his question clear.

She didn't say anything, but her eyebrow jutted down, and her jaw tightened as her eyes went hard, then flicked to Wallace's photo and back to the stack of papers in front of her.

Oh yeah, he would play poker with her anytime. She was easy to read. Not only did she purposefully not invite Trent, but she was angry at him about Wallace's death. But why?

Tom stepped up next to them, his expression haggard. "The preacher here has been kind enough to allow us to postpone until Tuesday at four. I sure hope that's enough time to get this case settled. Let's get those girls home before Alden haunts us all." He chuckled, though there was little joy in the sound.

Hoyt smiled, but a chill crawled up his spine.

There was something that still haunted them all from that night, and the number of ghosts on Shadow Island was growing.

13

"Viviane, can you start handing these out? Everyone has their routes already. Remember, folks, we want these posted as prominently as possible. But you cannot post them on private property without consent. You have to get permission from owners or managers at stores before you can hang them on their windows. There's plenty of tape to go around too. Greg, we've got a staple gun for you to hit up all the light poles."

Rebecca started pulling out stacks of "Have You Seen Me" flyers. The color photos stood out well, just as she'd expected. All three missing girls were featured. And below their original pictures were mockups the FBI had supplied if the girls had their appearances altered to look like boys.

"If you don't hang all your flyers, please bring them back, and we'll take them out ourselves. But the more we can get up and the faster we can do it, the more likely we are to find these girls. We want their faces everywhere."

A skinny teen wearing a white shirt shuffled up to her and took a roll of tape and a stack of flyers.

"Zack, thank you again for delivering all this. I know it

was last minute, but there are at least six parents out there tonight who will sleep better because of this. I know I will."

"I had to do something. I couldn't just look at these photos then go home. I've got a little sister. What if it had been her? She runs off while we're in town all the time. Now I get why Mom freaks out."

Rebecca looked down at the sweet, innocent faces and knew exactly what he was feeling. "Every missing child is someone's son, daughter, sister, brother. When it hits home, the world feels like a much scarier place." She grabbed his hand and waited 'til he lifted his scared eyes to meet hers. "But people like you are what brings them back to us."

She got a weak smile before he turned to rejoin his friends. Viviane, Greg, and Melody finished handing out the flyers. Meg gave Rebecca a little wave before heading out herself. She was going to be sitting with Mrs. Harper while Mr. Harper spread the flyers around the neighborhood.

As quickly as they showed up, everyone dispersed again. Hoyt had disappeared somewhere in the back, and Darian was riding out to the bridge to pick up the extra Explorer after kissing his wife goodbye. She hated asking Darian to leave his newborn to come in and work.

Thankfully, she shouldn't have worried. Once Mrs. Hudson had heard about what was going on, she'd urged him to go. The idea of someone's little girl being out there with traffickers while she cuddled her own baby had been too much for her to bear. If her own mother hadn't put a stop to it, she would have been out walking the streets with the rest of the volunteers.

Realizing that she was once again the only officer left, Rebecca handed the dispatch chair and headset over to Viviane and headed back to the office to do more grunt work. There was still so much video footage around Sylvie's abduction site to go through. This required a quick stop at the break station to grab a coffee and a bottle of eyedrops tucked into the first aid kit.

Eyes refreshed, and bolstered by the steaming cup of joe, she resigned herself to the computer desk once again. Set up with a notepad, pen, and her fingers ready to hit pause, she started watching all the compiled footage from all three abductions. Every vehicle that passed the cameras got a note to see if there were any that showed up at more than one location.

It was only a few minutes into some doorbell camera footage that she caught sight of what could be the van the Dixons had described seeing before their daughter had gone missing. She jotted down the parts of the license plate number she could make out. Before she could do any more than that, there was a knock on the doorframe.

"What's up?" She hit pause and looked up from her footage to see Hoyt standing there, a folder in his hands.

He opened his mouth to respond, closed it, then pinched his lips shut.

"Spit it out. Where'd you disappear to? We have hours and hours of footage to go through, and I need a few more sets of eyes on this if we're going to make any headway." She tried to read the label on the file, but Hoyt kept moving it as he seemed to be debating whether to show it to her.

"You knew." Hoyt clamped his mouth closed again, the muscle in his jaw jerking.

"I know lots of things. Lots of things I don't know. Could you be more specific?" Rebecca turned her attention back to the footage. She was certain she was making headway but needed to check the third abduction video.

Darian strode up beside him. "What's going on?"

Hoyt slapped the folder into Darian's chest. "Read this. Sheriff, what do you need help with?"

Though she was curious about what was in the folder, she

decided to ignore it for now. They'd all been through an emotional event, one she'd set up, and feelings were running high. Grief did weird things to people. She knew that first-hand, so she was going to give them as much room to grieve as possible.

"Grab the footage Viviane managed to cobble together from our local CCTVs. We're looking for a white Ford van with wide-angle side mirrors. I need to know where it went after leaving Bower Street."

Glancing up at Darian, she almost asked him to call Meg, then saw that he was busy frowning as he read over the file Hoyt had handed him. Instead, she hit the intercom button for Viviane.

"Yeah, Sheriff, you need something?"

"Can you call your mother, please? I don't want to tie up the Harpers' phones by calling them, but I need to speak with them."

"Sure, you want Mama to call you?"

"Yes, please, once she has both Harpers and can talk. Thank you."

"Sure. I'll get right on it."

Rebecca went back to the footage, hoping it would show her what she needed.

"Have you seen this?"

Rebecca had almost forgotten that Darian was still standing there. She'd been too focused on the footage playing past at high speed. She clicked pause again and looked up. "Seen what?"

He waved the folder at her. "This."

"Maybe if you would stop shaking it, I could read the label. Or you could just tell me so I can get back to tracking down the man who kidnapped Sylvie Harper."

Darian's hand tightened on the papers, and his jaw clenched, but he didn't say anything.

What the hell is going on?

Rebecca reached her hand out so he would pass over the file. Maybe then she'd finally understand what was bothering them both so much.

"Nothing, Sheriff. Sorry. I'll go help Frost now." Darian dipped his head before turning and rushing up the hallway.

Rebecca stared after him, but not for long. They were probably both pissed that she'd excluded Trent Locke from the ceremony, but hell...

Sighing, Rebecca backed the footage up a few frames and restarted it.

STILL REELING from what he'd just read, Deputy Darian Hudson made his way to the bullpen. "Frost, what the hell is this shit?" He slapped the file down on the first deputy's desk.

"Right?" Hoyt stopped what he was doing and turned to face the fuming man. "That's the official report. So at least Trent knew better than to lie when it counted."

"This is not what he told me happened." Darian's blood pounded as a mixture of anger and shame seethed around in his guts.

"Me neither."

Viviane hopped out of her seat and came scampering over. "What are we talking about? Is it gossip? I like gossip. Who are we gossiping about?"

Ignoring her, Hoyt pushed the folder back toward Darian. "Did you read the evidence report?"

"Evidence report?" Viviane wrinkled her nose. "That doesn't sound juicy at all."

"Oh, it's a regular watermelon, Darby," Hoyt assured her as Darian flipped through the pages and started to read the report as well. "*Trent* was Wallace's backup that night at the beach. Not West. She was the bait and took down the first guy, then the shooting started."

Viviane frowned. "Yeah, and…?"

Darian jerked his gaze up to stare at her. "You knew?"

Viviane shrugged. "Well, I was here when they were discussing how the trap should work. And that's what Wallace decided to do. Rebecca was sitting on the sand waiting for the boat while Trent and Wallace," she glanced over to the black-framed picture now hanging on the wall, "were supposed to hide on the other side of the dune in the old witch's cottage. Close enough to hear her but be hidden from sight. Wallace was worried about not being able to hear if the wind kicked up."

"Wallace went down pretty quickly." Hoyt ran a hand through his hair.

"And then Trent left him lying there, ran forward, and fired on the boat." Darian nearly choked on his anger. None of this was what Trent had told him had happened when he'd come over to visit his new daughter.

"That all sounds pretty scary. But why are you two so pissed about this?" Viviane leaned over Darian's shoulder and read along with him.

Darian scanned the words again. "Trent screwed up."

Every page he read, it just got worse and worse. Rebecca made the arrests, maintained the scene, filed the paperwork, coordinated with crime scene techs, and interrogated the guy she detained at the beach, getting him to admit to working with the Yacht Club. And…she was the one to administer first aid.

What the hell had Locke been doing?

Hoyt clarified. "From what I understand, Trent was supposed to cover Wallace and didn't. Then, when Wallace went down, Trent finally engaged in the firefight."

"He left our sheriff wounded and defenseless." The words were bitter in Darian's mouth.

Viviane looked confused. "What was he supposed to do? Administer first aid while bullets were flying?"

Darian knew it was a legitimate question, but his anger at how Locke told the story versus the reality of what had happened didn't sit right with him. "Still...if he screwed up by not covering Wallace properly, he should just own up to it instead of blaming everything on West."

Viviane nodded, her fingers pressed to her temples. "Very true."

"Plus, it was West who administered first aid." Darian leaned against the desk, shaking his head. "It was her shirt that was packed around his wound to stop him from bleeding out."

Hoyt reached over and yanked the file out from between Darian's hands. He flipped through it, then slammed a piece of paper down.

"Read this part."

Viviane, once again, leaned over his shoulder as he read through the autopsy report. Darian felt the blood drain from his face and cursed in a way that would've made his mother wash out his mouth, despite him being a grown man.

The bottom line was that Wallace could have been saved if treated more promptly.

If Locke had started first aid instead of swimming out to catch the drifting boat holding the dead shooter, their sheriff might still be alive. Hell, that was what the Coast Guard was for.

"I need a stiff drink," Viviane whispered, her fingers trembling where they covered her lips.

Darian's mind raced a mile a minute, and he felt like he couldn't breathe. He wanted to punch something, someone. *And the bastard would deserve it. Idiot!*

The rational side of him knew that Wallace's death wasn't Locke's fault. Not really. What pissed him off was how Locke had been badmouthing Rebecca ever since that terrible night. How did Trent think he could get away with this? Darian's hands dropped to his sides, and he blew out a breath. Now was not the time for him to lose his cool.

Viviane looked like she was about to be sick. Darian needed to get himself under control before she did. His anger would just make the situation worse.

Hoyt came back with a cup of cold water and pressed it into Viviane's hands. "Small sips. It'll make you feel better. Don't chug."

Viviane did as she was told. Her voice was barely audible when she spoke. "It's the witch's curse. I told him not to hide in that old cottage, but—"

"Viviane, honey, please don't start." Hoyt attempted to cut off her line of thinking, and Darian agreed. Now was not the time to entertain local legends. He dropped back into his seat. "This doesn't mean it's his fault—"

Darian held up a hand. "It does, however, mean that it's not *her* fault. Which is what he's been telling everyone."

"Oh, it gets better." There was a strange glint in Hoyt's eyes.

He was angrier than Darian had ever seen him. This was just getting worse and worse.

"He's not just spreading those rumors here. I got a call earlier from Lynnhaven PD. The chief there. He was told that Rebecca is *still* FBI, that she's *pretending* to be the sheriff. The chief called me because he thought *I* was the *real* sheriff."

"Son of a bitch." Darian threw his hands up and started pacing. He couldn't hold still. Not now. "I told him he needed to get over her holding the position for now. You can't do it. You're not off full medical leave. I can't do it. I've got a newborn I'm still trying to spend time with. He can't do it because—"

"Because Trent's an incompetent asshole who got our last sheriff killed because he couldn't follow standard operating procedure and..." Hoyt ran a hand down his face. "And he let him bleed out, which caused the stroke that killed him."

Viviane laid her head down on the desk and started to cry.

Darian swooped past Hoyt to comfort her. "Dammit, Frost."

Viviane sat up and leaned forward, hugging Darian as he stroked her hair.

Hoyt grimaced and rubbed her back. "I'm sorry. I didn't mean...you weren't...I'm sorry."

"Gentlemen!" Rebecca's voice rang out, making Darian jerk where he knelt. "What's going on out here?" She marched over.

Hoyt moved quickly, sitting on the paper he'd left on his desk.

"Sorry, Boss. We were talking about...about Wallace, and things got a little emotional."

Her face softened, and her pace slowed down a hair. "I should've guessed. Today's been rough on everyone. Viviane, do you need to go home?"

Viviane shook her head, wiping the tears off her cheeks. Darian smoothed her hair back from her face, checking her over as she pulled away from him, his paternal instincts in overdrive as his emotions warred under the surface.

"No. I'm sorry. It just got to me all of a sudden." She held up the glass of water and tried to smile. "I've got some water. I'll feel better soon."

"If you need to sit and have a cry, feel free to take the sheriff's office." Rebecca gave her friend a short hug, then turned her attention to Hoyt. "Did you manage to find either vehicle on the footage?"

Smiling at the change in topic, Hoyt nodded. "The blue sedan had the Harpers in it. Just them. They went to the beach, and everyone climbed out. I saw the whole thing. The white van disappeared in a blind spot, but I know exactly where it was. The only place it could go from there would be back into town, to one of the beach parking spots that's been closed off since it's so run-down, or to the beach itself. We know it didn't go to the beach because we canvassed that area, and there were no tracks in the sand."

Rebecca nodded. "Let's go check those parking lots then. That van was seen at all three abduction sites. More than likely, that's our guy." She started to turn away but stopped. "I need one of you to come with me."

Hoyt stood and moved to join her.

She frowned in thought. The look on her face made Darian uneasy, but he wasn't sure why. There was something...cunning and despicable in it. For a brief moment, he thought about how far she'd gone to get revenge for her parents. All he knew was what had been in the papers, but even that was enough to make him know he never wanted Rebecca West to be mad at him.

"Which one of you made Viviane cry?" she asked, tapping her bottom lip thoughtfully.

Darian pointed at Hoyt so fast his elbow popped, but he didn't care. He didn't want to carry that shame.

Viviane nodded and pointed at Hoyt too.

Hoyt gaped at them both, his jaw dropped. "Guys, come on..." He turned to Rebecca. "It wasn't like that. It was an accident. A thoughtless word and..." He trailed off, seeing the face that Darian had seen and been cowed by.

"Whatever it was like, you're now the one who gets to

stay here and clean the coffeepot. It tastes like shit. Hudson, you're with me."

Darian got up, grabbed his gun from his locked drawer, and put it in his holster. Racing around his desk, he gave Viviane one last pat and tossed a sympathetic smile Hoyt's way. He'd liked Rebecca from the first time he'd worked with her. Then he'd gotten angry at what he'd thought was her screwup. Now that he knew better, Darian was more than happy to be her backup again.

Darian loved Wallace, but it had been a long time since he'd followed someone like Rebecca. She was the type of stone heart he could learn from.

She headed for the door, snatching up the keys to a cruiser as she passed the desk.

Darian was right behind her.

"Frost," Rebecca called over her shoulder.

"Yeah, Boss?"

"You get to call Meg and explain to her why she heard her daughter crying while on the phone with me."

Darian flinched at that. Now he knew why his boss had had that scary expression on her face before she'd asked her question. She'd been planning something diabolical. He very happily followed the sheriff out of the station to the parking lot where there might be armed men hiding in a van. It would be much safer out there.

Because he knew Sheriff Rebecca West would have his back.

14

Darian drove, since he knew exactly where the parking areas Hoyt had described were located. He didn't say a word, which was fine with Rebecca.

She stared out the window at the long shadows leaning away from buildings and houses passing in a blur. It was evening now. Sylvie had been missing since that morning. Rebecca tried not to think about what could have happened to the child in that amount of time, but she'd seen too many crime scenes and even more photos to pretend she didn't know. As always, the unknown was what ate at her.

And they still had no firm leads. Nothing to direct the investigation. Hell, the agent she'd been promised by the FBI hadn't even shown up yet. Except for the backup from Coastal Ridge and highway patrol, no one she had called had shown up on land. The Coast Guard had, so that was a relief. The two ways off the island were protected as best as they could manage. With no direction to take, circling the wagons was the best they could do.

As long as the girl or girls were still on the island, of course.

One of the best parts of being a law enforcement officer on an island—it didn't take long to get anywhere. Rebecca hadn't even really had a chance to mire herself in dark thoughts before they were on a back road, and a small parking area tucked behind a tall row of beach grass came into view.

She let out a relieved breath. "Bingo."

It was the first parking lot they'd checked, and it contained a single vehicle. A white van with painted-over windows and wide-angle side mirrors, just like the Dixons had described.

Darian drummed his hands on the steering wheel. "Please tell me that's what I think it is?"

Rebecca realized that he had never actually seen any of the pictures or read the description since he'd come in so late. "It sure looks like it." The snap of her holster was loud in the confined space, and Darian glanced over at her before reaching for the radio.

"Dispatch, we've got eyes on the van. No one in sight. Pulling in now."

"Park at an angle in the driveway—"

"Blocking exit." Darian nodded, maneuvering the cruiser so her side faced the parking lot at an angle that would allow her protection behind her door if things went south. "Don't worry, Sheriff. I know how to follow SOP."

That sounded more important than it should, given the circumstances, but Rebecca wrote it off as the deputy assuring her that he had her back if things went sideways. She had no time to think about that, however. She opened the door. Even though she couldn't see anyone through the windshield, she grabbed her radio with her left hand and her gun with her right.

Bracing her gun hand on the back of her left wrist, she stepped out of the cruiser as soon as it stopped, leveling her weapon at the van. "This is the sheriff. Step out of the vehicle with your hands up!" She projected her voice as loudly as she could while ducking behind the open door.

"Sheriff's department." Darian's voice was more like a bark. "Hands where I can see them and exit the vehicle immediately!"

They waited a full fifteen seconds while nothing moved.

"Can you see any movement in the glass or mirrors?" Rebecca clipped her handheld radio to her pocket. "I don't have a full view."

"Can't see anyone in the driver or passenger's side, but they could be leaned over or in the footwell."

"Or in the back."

Rebecca was focused on the van while keeping her eyes wide to make sure nothing moved around them. This was a beach, after all, and anyone could be out enjoying the day, even if this was a rarely used location. The last thing she wanted was for an innocent bystander to get caught in the middle.

"This is the Shadow Island Sheriff. Exit the vehicle with your hands up!" In a lower voice, she called to the deputy. "Hudson."

Taking her direction and keeping low, Darian stepped around his door and moved toward the front of the cruiser, kneeling behind the front tire with his weapon braced on the hood.

"Sheriff." It was all he needed to say to let her know he was in position.

Her next move was riskier than his. Keeping her weapon trained on the driver's door of the van, she stepped around her own door and made her way to the vehicle.

A quick peek in the driver's side window confirmed that no one lurked in the front. She tried to see in the back windows, but they were just as opaque as they had appeared on the footage. Not a tint or one-way decal cover that could be seen through from the inside. She could see the streaks of a recent and rushed spray-paint job. That didn't bode well. This wasn't a vehicle a criminal would keep around for long.

When Rebecca was safely tucked in and waiting, Darian made his move, doing exactly as she had done but on the passenger side. As if they had trained together, they worked as a unit until they reached the back.

He shook his head. "Can't see shit."

This looked like a single-use vehicle. One that was ditched as soon as they were done using it and had no connection to the people who drove it last.

"Do we wait?" Darian put his hand flat on the back door, and she knew he was not only leaving a palm print just in case but also testing for any vibration that might indicate movement inside. "Nothing's moving."

Rebecca nodded. She'd leaned her shoulder against the tail-light to check as well. It seemed like the van was empty, but...

"If they're inside with Sylvie, we can't risk waiting for backup. We do this on three." When Darian nodded, she started the count. "One..."

Darian stayed at the back while she sidestepped to the side door. Once she got close enough, she grabbed ahold of the sliding door's handle. Not to open it, but to keep it from being opened before she was ready.

"Two...three!"

Jerking the handle, she slid open the side door, gun ready. The back door opened as well, and Darian appeared, his gun steady in his hands. They cleared the back of the empty van, seeing only blankets.

She opened her mouth to speak, then stopped as she smelled something unexpected. "Come around and tell me if I'm insane or if I'm really smelling what I think I'm smelling."

Darian headed her way, his eyes moving back and forth, the same as hers were, checking the area around them.

"I never like it when someone asks me to smell something. Especially on scene. It never ends well."

She smirked, knowing exactly what he meant. There had been way too many times she'd smelled gut-churning things on the job. And this was essentially a big metal box that had sat in the sun for the last couple of hours, so whatever was inside had marinated and baked in the heat, becoming even more pungent.

"This one might surprise you."

Darian leaned in, holstering his gun, and took a deep breath through his nose. He frowned, sniffed again, then leaned in more, taking another deep breath, his eyebrows furrowing.

Now that she was sure the scene was secure, Rebecca holstered her weapon. "Am I right?"

"Is that...wet dog?"

"That's what I thought. But more like puppy. Wet puppy, and I thought I smelled urine too." Rebecca reached into her back pocket, where she'd stowed a baggie of gloves before leaving the station. She pulled out a pair and put them on. "Call this in and get forensics out here too."

Gloved up, Rebecca reached for the blanket just inside the door and lifted it. The smell of wet dog got even stronger, and there was loose golden fur embedded all through the blanket's coarse weave. Something fell out of the blanket with a soft thump. Looking down, Rebecca saw a small orange object and picked it up.

"This is the vehicle used to kidnap Sylvie Harper." She held up the nub of orange chalk and showed it to Darian. "She was drawing with chalk on the sidewalk the last her father saw her."

"And they used the old puppy trick to get her in the van?" Darian wrinkled his nose.

There was a reason parents warned their children about the ruse. It was old and well-known, but it worked surprisingly well even still. Puppies were just too irresistible to some children, especially animal lovers like little Sylvie.

"Looks like." A quick glance under the driver's seat revealed something new. A blue hat with a white bird on the front. "Bingo."

Darian frowned at the cap. "Bingo how?"

Rebecca recounted the description Evelyn Dixon had provided of the man she'd noticed before her daughter Chelsea was taken. "Let's bag it and send it off for possible DNA analysis."

Darian held out a bag. "Good find."

While the deputy labeled the evidence bag, Rebecca walked around to the back of the van and jotted down the license plate number. Considering the paint job on the windows, she wasn't expecting much good would come of running the plate, but it needed to be checked anyway. If it came up stolen, like she assumed it would, it would still give them another location to investigate based on where it was taken from.

While Darian made the call on the radio, Rebecca walked back to the cruiser and punched the new information into the laptop. The sooner they could get this update out, the better. She heard Darian doing what she had asked and listened to the response. Forensics had been waiting on standby and were already on their way. They should be there in just a few minutes.

Just like I planned. Perfect. Now to check the plate.

Entering the number into the computer, she wasn't surprised but was disappointed when it came back stolen. From Chincoteague, Virginia, another island town. Taken from a beachside parking lot. Yet another commonality to every case.

Rebecca got back out of the cruiser. Darian was still on the radio, setting everything up. Walking around the empty lot, Rebecca checked for any other evidence.

Sand had blown into the parking lot and was layered fairly thick in spots. There was a nice layer of it in the space next to the van. Which only had one mark on it. A single set of tire tracks. A quick look at the van showed it wasn't the same tread.

Waving her hand, she caught Darian's attention, then pointed to the tracks in the sand. He nodded, indicating he understood and wouldn't walk there, destroying their evidence. Still, Rebecca kept her patrol small, keeping the piece of evidence in sight at all times.

There were no other prints in the sand around the lot, nor anything else she could see that would be useful.

Darian finished up his calls, and Rebecca walked over. "They're targeting tourists. Either because they know the tourists are easy marks, out drinking and partying, or because they know the cops won't want to make it known that tourists are being targeted when the cities rely on tourism money. Either way, it's an easy and wide market for them to pick from."

"Sounds about right, considering where all the crimes are happening. Or it could be that they're on the water."

Rebecca struggled to get the radio clip off her pocket, the loose fabric catching on the hook.

Darian shook his head. "Civvy clothes aren't meant for this kind of thing."

She grumbled.

He laughed in agreement.

"Abner, you got your ears on?"

Greg responded immediately. "Yeah, Sheriff, I'm here. What's up?"

Rebecca frowned. The guys all seemed to be calling her *sheriff* now, and she wasn't sure why. Or if she liked it. This was just a short-term gig for her until someone, anyone, else could take over. While she appreciated the professional respect, she didn't want them to get used to it. "We're at Atticus Beach. Did your guys check out the water around here?"

"That where the van was found?"

"Yes. And where I think Sylvie was transferred. We've got a second set of tire tracks here. But I want to verify that there was no other vehicle in the area. We don't have any tracks on the beach, but still…"

"Yeah, there's good fishing there in the morning. Ryker was there from dawn 'til when I called him to come help. He said it was dead, didn't catch a single fish but also didn't see another boat. 'Course, he couldn't see the lot past the dunes."

Ryker? Could it be her Ryker? Not like he was hers, but…

"Well, that at least lets us know they didn't get off the island here, if Ryker was here that early." Pondering her nonexistent social life would have to come later.

Having already checked the ground, Rebecca raised her eyes and continued her search. There, just behind the sodium light on one of the poles, was what she had hoped to find. A surveillance camera.

Tourist towns can be counted on for more than just easy marks.

"Thanks, Greg. Viviane, there's a camera out here too. Think you can pull up the footage?"

"Yeah, I'm sitting here ready. Got all the folders open and ready to be searched through. I got you, boo."

Had she heard that right? "Boo?"

"Boo-oss." Viviane giggled at her own humor.

Rebecca had to take a moment to decide if she should tell

Viviane to calm down with the jokes. After all, she had gotten onto Hoyt for gossiping on the radio a few hours ago.

She didn't get the chance.

"Hey, you know the last time I had to pull up this footage was when that man got drunk and spray-painted a penis on the asphalt."

"I don't need that kind of footage." Rebecca shook her head. Maybe what she'd heard this morning wasn't that unusual from their normal chatter. Maybe Rebecca needed a better sense of humor?

Not now.

A shiny white van headed up the road toward them, and Rebecca walked back to the cruiser. "Okay, everyone, forensics just pulled up. If this is the van used to abduct Sylvie, we need to be ready to move forward quickly. Darian, can you check if our theories are right about this being a secondary scene?"

"Roger that, Boss."

Rebecca was still shaking her head as she got into the cruiser to move it out of the way for the forensics van. She hoped the little levity they'd gotten to enjoy would be enough to carry them through whatever the techs found in the back of the vehicle.

Please don't let there be any bodily fluids.

15

"That'll teach the little shits."

The girls would keep their traps shut now. I tossed the phone book down with a satisfied smile.

All satisfaction disappeared when my phone rang. It could only be one person.

That wasn't good. There was no reason for her to be calling. Not now. Not unless she was trying to worm her way into my retirement plans again. Fat chance of that ever happening. Once this was over, I planned to leave her and her bullshit behind.

In a body bag, preferably.

I yanked my phone out.

The bitch didn't even give me a chance to speak before blurting, "Everything's falling apart."

So dramatic.

"What happened?" I faked a yawn to show her how little I cared. "Bartender cut you off already?"

"No, you idiot. This is bad. Awfully bad."

Granted, she seemed sincere in her hysteria this time.

Was I ready to jump on the crazy train with her, though? Not hardly.

"What's bad?"

"I had everything all planned so perfectly. The sheriff's funeral is supposed to be this evening, which is why I scheduled for us to leave the island tonight."

Why was she telling me this again?

"Yes, I know. It's the way *we* planned it, remember?"

"Well, guess what? Instead of all the locals drowning in their sorrows and not paying attention to what's going on in their community, they've got cops from other areas conducting DUI checks at the bridge. Even the highway patrol is out there with a damn dog. A couple of people were complaining about it, so I drove by to see for myself. They're checking every car."

Hm…that wasn't good, but it wasn't the end of the world either. We'd planned the third snatch on a day the local cops wouldn't be patrolling the roads. They'd never notice me driving three little girls to the second staging area. We'd be off the island in plenty of time for the drop-off.

"We'll just wait 'til the checkpoint is over. Those only last a couple of hours. Just keep drinking until you pass out and trick some local asshole into making the worst decision of his year. What's the big deal?"

"What's the big deal?" Her voice went up several octaves. "Are you stupid?"

I ground my teeth together. This was why I hated talking to the bitch over the phone. She wouldn't dare say shit like that to my face, knowing I would slap the nasty right out of her mouth. Over the phone, I couldn't touch her.

"Don't call me stupid. Especially not when you're freaking out over a nonissue like a couple hours of delay when we don't even have anyone waiting for us yet. The exchange isn't even until the day after tomorrow, right? Because *you* decided to snag the kid early, we have to sit on more kids for longer because no one is ready to pick them up yet!"

My plan had been to wait until the day after tomorrow and just snatch the kid before driving straight over the bridge. Easy breezy. But no, the bitch had insisted we get the girl early, thinking it would give me time to get her settled into her new life before the buyer took them over.

Me. I was the one now responsible for babysitting children instead of my wife. Why? Because she was becoming such a lush that she couldn't be trusted.

It hadn't always been this way. When we'd first met, we were like Bonnie and Clyde. We'd plotted and implemented our plans with an ease that often felt like a miracle. Then, the booze took over and started scrambling her brain. If she hadn't had so much evidence on me, I would've gotten rid of her a long time ago.

It was the evidence that kept me hooked to her, dammit.

Pictures of me with the kids. Several videos too. Videos where I'd taken too much interest in the older girls.

Yeah…I was fucked.

So here I was, trying to reason with a drunk who held my life in her hands.

"Are you really this thick?" she shrieked through the phone. "If I remember correctly, you're the asshole who wanted to come down to this island to find the last one. Now you're stuck there. Don't blame me!"

Of course I'd wanted to come here for the last pickup. It was where my safe house was, but she didn't need to know that. I needed a place to put the first two kids while I waited for the perfect opportunity to take the third.

"I do blame you." The words were more snarl than anything, and I forced myself to take a breath. This wasn't getting us anywhere. I needed to control this conversation. "Listen, let's both calm down and think it all through."

Her exhale blew static into my ear. "Okay. Have you listened to the news?"

I relaxed with her calmer tone. Hating to admit that I hadn't paid the news much attention in the past few hours, I only grunted in response.

Ice clinked in a glass. She was, in fact, drinking again. Shocker. "The Amber Alert hit quicker than the first two did."

That got my attention, and I reached for my phone. I hadn't taken it in with me while I was punishing the girls and could have missed something important. "What did the alert say? Anything about who snatched her? Anything that could identify me?"

"No." Tammy took a noisy slurp of her drink. "It was standard description and shit. But get this, they've somehow linked this snatch with the other two."

Shit.

That meant the power of the law times three were currently putting their collective heads together searching for me.

I really do need to retire.

"How?"

It was a stupid question, I knew, but I'd been lucky in the past skating by these Podunk police punks. Why wasn't I skating by them now?

Had I gotten too cocky? Maybe. But the biggest reason we were in this mess right now was on the other side of this phone call.

I needed to kill her.

Not just think about it but follow through. She and her evidence against me would be officially gone from my life, and I'd get her share of the money.

"...are you listening to me?"

Snapping my mind away from my musings, I realized I'd

completely zoned her out. It wasn't hard. I'd had years of practice. "I'm thinking. Give me a minute."

She didn't, of course. "They're going to find you with them! That means no money."

"No. I won't let it come to that. If they get too close, I'll slit their throats and get away." I began to pace. "If you'd brought more than a single dose of ketamine, I could just knock them out and toss them in the trunk under some blankets."

She scoffed and took an enormous drink. "That sniffer dog will rat you out in ten seconds if you do that." Her words were beginning to slur.

Apprehension wrapped around me like a wet blanket. "Let me tell you something right now, bitch. You better not be planning to pin all of this on me again. Because I swear to you right now, if I get caught, I'm telling them all about you. And your plan. How you set this all up and even handpicked the merchandise. I'll tell them I knew nothing about it and was just helping you move a car."

"You bastard."

"Eat shit. You think I'm gonna let you ruin my life? I have the merchandise. You need me."

"You wouldn't cut me out, would ya?" she asked in that sweet little voice she'd used on me back in the day. Though the drunken slur took most of its power away. "After everything we've been through? You still need one last payday, and you know I'm good at finding buyers. Come on."

Two could play this game.

"Don't worry, sugar bear." I made my voice as sugary sweet as hers. "I bet they won't have any real evidence against *you*. They won't be able to convict *you*. *You'll* just have to spend a little time behind bars, but that's nothing. Right?" I barked a laugh. "Isn't that what you said just before we got caught and you turned on me?"

Silently, I enjoyed the image of her mouth opening and closing like a fish.

Finally, she sputtered, "I'm calling McGuire. Telling him what's up and see what he wants to do. If we need to drug the girls again so soon, he needs to know."

She couldn't be serious.

"You do that and—"

The line went dead. That empty-headed bitch had hung up on me.

I snatched a beer. Of course it wasn't cold anymore. Regardless, I popped the top and downed half the bottle. I set it back down. I needed to keep a clear head and chugging the rest wouldn't do it.

My *darling* wife—I gritted my teeth at the phrase—would spend the rest of the evening sitting at a bar, drinking her fruity cocktails, and flirting with whatever man looked her way, while I got us out of this mess. She was as loyal as a dandelion seed. Moving any which way the wind blew.

I had to make sure she knew I wouldn't bite my tongue this time. I had picture and video proof on her too. If I was going down, I'd take her with me. That thought kept me from getting too riled up until she called me back.

The ringtone barely sounded before I answered. "Yeah?"

"McGuire understands. He's not worried, but he's sending a man to meet you. He's going to check the merchandise. If everything looks good, we'll hand it over there. I just need the address for where you're staying."

My address? To my safe house? The one I'd kept secret for years now? No one knew where it was. "Have them send a boat instead. There's a private beach nearby. I'll take the girls down there and hand them over."

"No way." Not quite that stupid, she pushed back. "I'm not trusting you to take the money. I'd never see my split."

She was right, but it'd been worth a shot.

"I—"

"Besides, there's Coast Guard all over the place. They might be running practice drills, but I doubt it. They're moving up and down the coast. Everyone's been talking about how much they're messing up the waves, and no one can ski with them circling like this."

I bit my lip and rubbed my forehead. "You didn't tell McGuire about them, did you?"

"No, I didn't think to. Why would he care about some skiers?"

What. A. Stupid. Bitch.

Why did I get involved with her again? Oh, right, because she could suck the chrome off a trailer hitch. But it was more than that. We were both willing to do whatever it took to make a penny. Didn't find many women like that.

I ran through my options. If I gave away this address, I might not be able to use it again. But if this went through, I wouldn't need to use it again anyway. And if I didn't give up the address, then I wouldn't get this over with and the product sold ASAP.

What then?

I kill them and walk away with nothing? Give up on my plans?

No. This could be a good thing. I would sell out everything I had here, so there would be no turning back, and finally end this career.

"You got a pen?"

"I got a smartphone, dumbass. Tell it to me, and I'll text it right over to McGuire."

Reminding myself I could always kill her after this was all over, I told her the address. A pang of loss I wasn't expecting ran through me, but I ignored it. It was time to cut the deadweight and move on.

"Okay, I sent it. He should be there in an hour, max."

"Are you coming with him?" I held my breath, praying she'd say no.

She scoffed. "No. McGuire will make sure I get my share."

Just like Tammy. Afraid to get her hands dirty.

"Whatever. Just tell him to make sure he's not followed, and to park around back. There's a blue Intrepid back there. And knock twice. Otherwise, he's getting a stomach full of buckshot."

I didn't actually have a shotgun, but it was best to make them worry. It would keep them from acting stupid.

"Yeah, yeah. I'll tell him. Just don't do anything stupid."

"I—"

The line went dead.

Over the next half hour, I thought about how nice it would be to give myself a clean break. To make sure the break was completely clean, I needed to get rid of anything that would tie me to my previous jobs. None of my buyers knew my real name. Only she did.

I needed to get rid of her.

I had to. The bitch would find me and turn me over to the authorities no matter how far I fled.

As much as I didn't want to be taken into custody by the local cops, I really didn't want to be taken into custody by the Federales. During my stint in prison, I'd heard plenty of stories about how everything, especially the food, was so much cleaner here in the States.

I'd never asked how the food in Mexican prisons was dirty. I didn't want to know. And I planned to never find out. Yeah, it could have been them just hazing me, but I refused to risk it. Not for anything.

As I waited, I settled on a plan. I'd take the bitch out for drinks to celebrate, get her good and drunk, then take her out on a boat ride to Mexico. Dumped in the middle of the ocean for shark food was the perfect ending for a bitch-fish like her.

The knock on the door jarred me out of my wonderful daydreams of watching the mouthy whore drown in clear water. I waited, then a second knock followed.

Damn, the man was big. From the waist up, that was.

Tall, wearing a tank top that showed off all the muscles in his chest. And he had dull, dead eyes and thin lips. Typical. I'd seen plenty of guys just like him in prison. They worked out religiously, but only their upper bodies. So they could pummel the guy next to them before they got pummeled. Yeah, I knew his type. He was the muscle.

"McGuire sent me."

No shit.

"Yeah, come on in." I glanced into the backyard. Just as I'd instructed, he'd parked right next to my car but hadn't blocked me in. He'd also pulled in straight instead of backing in, like I had. This was a guy who followed orders but didn't think ahead. Even better.

I pulled the door closed behind him. He glanced around, taking everything in. Muscle man was also packing and not trying to hide it.

"Boss said I was to check the merch. Make sure you got it all."

I nodded, waving for him to follow me.

"You didn't touch 'em, did ya? Boss says they're supposed to be unspoiled for the buyers. That's what they want."

"No, I didn't touch 'em. Haven't even opened the door except to add the new one. All three are in the same room." I pointed at the door and handed him the key.

Muscles walked over and tested the deadbolt. Then, with his hand on his gun, he slowly opened the door. Maybe he wasn't smart or forward-thinking, but he wasn't dumb either. That could be a good or a bad thing.

I walked closer, just in case I had to catch any of the brats trying to escape.

But the big man was good for something, at least. All the crying and whimpering stopped the second he walked into the room.

Stepping into the doorway, I watched him. He walked up to each girl, looking them over as they huddled on the floor.

The new girl considered glaring at him but dropped her head and covered her face instead.

Muscles bent over and snatched her up by her wrist. Dangling from one arm, the girl cried out. Muscles lifted her straight up until she hung in front of his face. He twisted her around, inspecting every inch, and even smirked as she kicked her legs.

"Just checking for blood. The others look fine too."

I wasn't sure if he was talking to me or the girls. Either way, I had to exert some authority. "If you mark her up, I'm not taking any blame for that, and you're not going to lower the price."

Muscles shrugged and set the girl back down, where she collapsed into a ball and blubbered into her knees.

"I'll let the boss know if there're any issues, but bruises on the wrists are okay. Just not the face or other parts of the body. You gotta restrain 'em, after all. I didn't squeeze hard, anyway."

His job done, Muscles turned and walked out of the room.

I made sure he closed and locked the door, then waited as he made the call. I listened carefully to a series of "yeah, boss."

It was maddening.

When Muscles tucked his phone into his pocket, I held out my hand and waited until he handed the key back.

"McGuire says we're a go. We've got a vehicle that will get

through the checkpoint. With the damn dog sniffing every car, we have to take some extra precautions. I brought some scent-eliminating spray. Boss is bringing a refrigerated box truck with a load of citrus in it. We'll douse the kids with the spray and then stow them in the reefer truck. That way, we can take them tonight instead of waiting. It's risky, but McGuire says it's best to get this settled and get out of here."

I couldn't agree more.

Muscles leaned against the wall, arms crossed, staring straight ahead.

I went back to my wonderful daydream of what would be the last date with my wife. Widowers always got more tail anyway.

Damn, I should have held onto a puppy.

16

Hoyt started watching video footage from the small parking area as soon as Viviane added it to the digital case file on the shared drive. He might not always understand how this new tech worked, but he did appreciate how much easier and faster it made his job.

His screen was dark at first, making him wonder if the streetlight holding this video camera was out. He ran the footage faster, watching as the night brightened into a beautiful sunrise that would have taken his breath away had he not been on a mission.

The camera was part of their new Green Initiative. It captured high-definition color footage, with a two-hundred-and-seventy degree bird's-eye view. It was leaps and bounds better than the grainy, black-and-white film of the past.

As daylight broke more completely, Hoyt got his first good view of the parking lot. It was barely big enough to fit half a dozen cars and was just far enough away from the beach that the lot was often deserted, aside from a few locals who knew the shortcut down to the sand. It hadn't been deserted today.

It wasn't the white van Rebecca and Darian found earlier, though. Instead, a blue Intrepid sat as a lone sentinel facing the road. Peering closer, Hoyt couldn't detect any movement or human-shaped shadows inside. With no front plates or any other identifiable objects on the vehicle, he had little to go on.

He pressed the fast-forward button and watched as the morning sped past. At around the eight thirty mark—about two hours before Joseph Harper had last seen his daughter—Greg Abner rolled his chair over to sit beside him, dropping Wallace's case file on the corner of Hoyt's desk.

"Thanks for clueing me in." Greg patted him hard on the shoulder. "That's not what I wanted to know about what happened, but it's better than believing a lie."

Having spent entirely too much of his career kept in the dark about important matters, Hoyt nodded and pushed the file aside, keeping his attention on the screen. "I think it's about time we stopped letting rumors dictate how to run our island."

Greg blew out a long breath. "You think the new boss will make that happen?"

Hoyt messed with the video settings so he could watch it at ten times the normal speed and shrugged. "Does she seem like the type of person who hides from the ugly truth?"

With a grunt that ended in a chuckle, Greg shook his head. "Nope. She put up with us calling her by her first name this whole time and didn't seem to give a damn. She knew we didn't like her, and she just kept showing up and doing her job."

"Don't know about you, but that's the kind of person I'd like to see take the lead. Of any job, but especially ours. She's not afraid to get down in the trenches either." Hoyt motioned at the folder. "Played bait, no problem, even when she already thought the Yacht Club was a more dangerous issue than any of the rest of us did." His mind jumped back to the plaque that was now hanging on the wall of their lobby. "Integrity, honor, and commitment."

Greg grunted in agreement. Once word of the postponed funeral had gotten out, they'd had a slow trickle of mourners coming in to leave flowers, say prayers, or view the small memorial that had been set up. Without another word, Greg got up and made his way over to the counter.

"Hey."

Glancing away from the screen for only an instant, Hoyt looked over to where Greg was holding out a piece of paper. "What?"

"Check this out."

Hoyt frowned. He didn't have time for that.

When he didn't move, Greg walked back and waggled the paper in Hoyt's face.

Hoyt snatched it away and tossed it down. If he missed anything important on the screen, he would never forgive himself. "You either watch this video or read me whatever you think is so important."

With a sigh, Greg picked up the paper again. "It's a receipt for the picture and frame, billed to Rebecca West."

Hoyt frowned but didn't look away. "She paid for this out of her own pocket?"

"Yup." Greg sat back down. "I've ordered late-night dinners and office supplies often enough to know that's not our account number. She paid with her own credit card, out of her own pocket. To honor our sheriff without taking credit for it. A man she barely even knew."

Tears welled in the backs of Hoyt's eyes, and he let out a deep breath. That was something Alden would have done as well. This day was just a roller coaster of emotions, as Angie would say. "Wallace chose well when he asked her to help us."

"Yup, I reckon—"

"Wait." Hoyt slowed the video down to normal speed as a white van pulled into the parking area.

Leaning in, he reached for a pad and pen, ready to jot down time stamps and notes.

He watched as the van backed in and parked to the left of the Intrepid and waited. A few minutes later, a tan sedan pulled in, parking next to the left of the van, so their back doors lined up. Hoyt sat up straighter. They'd done this before.

From the angle of the shot, he couldn't see more than a person's head as he climbed out and hoisted Sylvie Harper's limp form onto his shoulder. Hoyt's guts turned to ice as he watched the way her body flopped around as she was carelessly transferred to the back seat of the Intrepid, not the new arrival.

After the man tossed Sylvie into the car like a sack of potatoes, the sedan's trunk—a Nissan Altima—popped up. The man went back to the van and pulled a bundle of something from the cargo area.

Hoyt cursed and zoomed in. Beside him, Greg leaned forward. "Is that the pup?"

Wrapped in a blanket, a few spots of pale fur stuck out in places. "Looks that way." The puppy was placed inside the trunk more carefully than the girl had been treated.

"Son of a bitch." As he watched, Hoyt allowed a few more expletives to slip out.

"What's that?"

Hoyt was already shaking his head, leaning closer to the screen. "It's a bag of...something." He tried to read the logo on the pink bag the man took from the trunk but couldn't. "Something *treasure*, maybe?"

Less than a minute later, the man got into the Intrepid and drove away. As hard as he looked, Hoyt couldn't see the plates.

"Damn." It was Greg's turn to curse. "I bet we'll see the other one since it didn't back in."

Saying a prayer, Hoyt held his breath as the video continued to play. "Come on. Let me see the driver and the plates."

The Altima backed up, did a three-point turn, with the driver being nothing more than a shadow. Then...the money shot. The license plate was right there for all to see.

Hoyt froze the video, grabbed a screenshot, and switched tabs. A search of the plate number connected it with the car it was attached to. And, surprisingly, it didn't come back as stolen. He pulled up the registration information.

Greg pointed at the screen. "Looks like you got something."

"Got the second car and plate. Found the registered owner too. Lorene Espry from Chincoteague, Virginia. Tan Nissan Altima. Not reported stolen."

Greg settled back in his chair and leaned in to read over Hoyt's shoulder. "What do we know about her?"

"Let's see." He clicked around a bit. "No criminal record and, oh...she's deceased."

"Suspicious."

Hoyt nodded. "It sure is. Let me check for the next of kin." A few more clicks led him to a birth certificate. "Got a daughter. Tammy Espry."

He went down a few rabbit holes before finding a marriage certificate. "Tammy Espry is now Tammy Carr."

Greg scratched his chin. "Why does that name sound familiar?"

A minute later, Hoyt rubbed his hands together. "Because she's married to Jon Carr, who has an extensive criminal record."

"A real love match. You dig into him, I'll dig into her." Greg rolled over to his desk and started his own search.

"Get this. Jon Carr was arrested for kidnapping three years ago. Two girls from Chincoteague and one from a neighboring town. But in the end, the charges were dropped due to lack of evidence." Hoyt jotted down the detective's name from the file and went looking for his contact information.

"What happened to the girls?"

He turned, his eyebrows raising in a shrug. "Doesn't say…"

"Yeah, well, get this." Greg waved his hand at his computer. "The loving wife gave an interview to the local paper. In it, she talks about how she doesn't know if Jon is capable of such dastardly things but claims she hasn't been with him in years. They married young, lost a child, and never recovered from that loss. They separated and are only technically married now, as neither one of them wanted to end their marriage but couldn't live together due to the over-whelming pain of their loss. *'He was a good man who started hanging out with a rough crowd after losing his only child.'*" He held both hands up to make finger quotes for the last part.

"Mmhmm. Or she's involved and playing innocent. His driver's license has the same address as her home address."

"Hard to be separated when you still live together." Greg's snide remark spoke volumes.

"I wonder if there's any extra information we can get." Hoyt picked up the phone. He dialed the number for Chincoteague PD, then waited while he was routed to the detective's number.

"Detective Sander. How can I help you?"

At Greg's frantic hand gestures, Hoyt put the call on speakerphone. "Detective Sander, this is Deputy Frost calling from Shadow Island. I was wondering if you could help me out."

"What can I do you for, Deputy?" The man sounded more than a bit distracted.

"I need information on Jon Carr and—"

"That son of a bitch? Yeah, I know the bastard. Spent three weeks hunting him down before I found him hiding two towns over, camping out in a foreclosed warehouse. He swore up and down he had no idea why we would be looking for him and that he never did nothing wrong." The detective's tone went dark. "Do you have missing girls down there?"

"Yes. Three of them. One locally, two from nearby towns."

"Dammit. That sounds like what we went through too. I knew this was going to happen one day. Give me your email address, Deputy Frost. I'll send you everything I have. In my bones, I knew this guy was guilty, but I got some evidence tossed due to ridiculous technicalities, and the case fell apart. I never found those girls."

"What do you think happened to them?"

Sander cleared his throat. "My line of thinking is he sold them. I don't think he took them for himself. We dug into everyone in his life, but we didn't find any connections that led anywhere."

An idea was forming in Hoyt's head but didn't yet have legs. "What about his wife? Do you think she had anything to do with your case?"

"His wife? What was her name? Cammy, something like that? She wasn't involved. There were plenty of eyewitnesses putting her in a bar at the times of the abductions. Others corroborated that he never visited her home during that time. She told us that they were separated and that he used her address for mail, but they hadn't been in contact for years."

"Hmm, well, I've got footage of her car meeting up with a

van used in an abduction. Our missing girl wasn't placed in her vehicle, but the puppy that was used to lure the girl was."

"I'll be a...we never did figure out how he transported the girls. He didn't have a vehicle that we could find. There wasn't one at the warehouse when we caught him. That was also a major hole the dick's defense attorney blew in our case." They both went quiet. Only the sound of flipping papers came through. "Deputy, can I call you right back? I need to check something."

"Yeah, of course, but can you hurry? We're hoping we've got them trapped on the island, and we want to get Sylvie safely home to her parents as soon as possible."

"Absolutely. Keep an eye on your inbox. I'll send over everything I have on both of them."

The line went dead, and Hoyt and Greg were left staring at each other.

Greg gave him a thumbs-up. "I think you just broke his case open."

"Could be. That would be good and all, but I want to nail Carr for these kidnappings first. Can't try him again for the other ones. Double jeopardy."

"You need to update the sheriff. Let her know what's going on."

"You're right. Let me text her." Hoyt tapped on his phone before redirecting his attention to Greg. "I wish we could've seen the plate on that Intrepid. The van was stolen but if we had those numbers, it would help with a BOLO."

"Pretty smooth system they've got going on, splitting up like that." Greg nodded. "I'm going to see if I can find out any more about our *innocent* grieving wife of the year."

That made Hoyt think of something else, but he lost that train of thought when Viviane called out, "Yes, can I help you, sir?"

Viviane had developed an easy way of letting everyone in

the station know when trouble showed up. She simply projected her voice loud enough to be heard in the bullpen and used an unnaturally professional tone. It was what she called her "customer service persona."

Hoyt stood and headed her way.

Whoever he was, he was a federal agent of some kind. If the navy jacket he wore didn't give it away, the short-cropped hair, standard black pants, and white shirt surely did. Worse, he didn't look old enough to drive a car.

"I'm Agent Christopher Stalwart from the FBI. We got a call about a possible kidnapping." He spoke without even bothering to look at Viviane, his eyes flitting around the lobby and casually sweeping over the memorial and the stack of gifts that had been left there.

"Not possible," Hoyt corrected as he walked up to the desk. He already didn't like this man. And not just because he didn't like outsiders coming in and taking over his case. Well…maybe that had a little bit to do with it.

But this guy exuded an arrogance that pissed Hoyt off.

"What's not possible?" Those lazy eyes flicked over to him, took in the uniform, and moved on.

"It's not a 'possible' kidnapping. It's a child abduction, and it matches two other child abductions that took place within the last few days in nearby towns."

The agent shifted his eyes back to Hoyt. "We'll see about that."

Viviane stayed still, but the rigid set of her back told Hoyt she liked this agent even less than he did.

"I assume you're the man in charge here? I need to see any reports you have."

"You're not good at making assumptions or putting pieces together. See, I'm a deputy." Hoyt tapped his name tag on his chest. "And this is a sheriff's office. If you want to see the person in charge, that would be the sheriff. Unfortunately for you, the sheriff's a bit busy right now at a secondary crime scene."

Agent Stalwart's nostrils flared. "But you're at least capable of compiling a few pieces of paper, right? If you can fetch those for me, I can tell you if this is an actual abduction or just a lost kid." The Feebie tried throwing the snark back at him but wasn't very good at it.

"I can, but I won't. If you want—"

"Look, if you want the FBI to take over this case for you, you need to at least give us what you have. Or don't you have anything?" He raised an eyebrow wrought with disdain.

Hoyt shifted his weight as Greg sauntered up behind him. Not to act as backup but to get a better view of what was about to go down.

"You're not here to take over anything. Let me make that clear, especially if you've come in here thinking we don't even have a kidnapped child. We don't have time to convince you otherwise. We have suspects and are closing in on where the children are being held. You can help us or get out of our way." *You don't even think there're kidnapped children?* Hoyt didn't say it, but he knew everyone in the room was thinking it too.

The agent crossed his arms over his chest. "If you didn't want us to take over this case, then why did you bother contacting us?"

"It's called standard operating procedure. See, when there're crimes that are linked or happen in more than one state, you have to notify the Effing BI. And since you seem to need a refresher on how law enforcement works, I'll also go ahead and explain it to you. All the files are linked in the NCIC. If you want to read what we have, log in yourself."

Hoyt spun the monitor on a nearby desk around, forcing himself not to wince as the movement pulled at his incision.

He knew he was handling this badly, but dammit...no one had time for this nonsense.

"I'll do that right after I speak to Sheriff, um..."

Hoyt held back a curse. "West. And you'll find her at the secondary crime scene, working her ass off to find those children."

"Where is this scene located?"

Viviane jotted the information down and handed it to the agent. "It's where all the fancy cars with the flashing lights are. You probably passed it on your way here," Viviane added helpfully, with a dazzling smile that didn't reach her eyes or hide her mocking tone.

Pinching his lips tight, the agent spun on a heel, showing off the bright yellow letters on the back of his jacket, and stormed out the door.

Viviane wrinkled her nose, looking a bit contrite. "Think we should warn Rebecca that we pissed off a Fed?"

Greg snorted. "Nah, she's got this."

17

Rebecca rubbed the back of her neck and stood up to stretch. She'd been following the techs as they pulled the van apart while waiting for the mold of the tire track to cure enough that she could get a good look at it. Under better conditions, they would have just taped the whole thing up and taken it back to an evidence locker. But with the situation they were in now, every moment counted. Traffickers were known to dispose of their cargo if they thought the police were closing in.

Cargo. Merchandise. Shipment.

All terms traffickers used to describe the people they stole away from their loved ones. They were also terms law enforcement ended up using just so they wouldn't go mad with worry thinking about an eight- or nine-year-old girl crying for her mommy.

For different reasons, having to resort to using those terms always turned Rebecca's stomach. That was something she hoped would never stop happening. She'd made a vow back in her academy days that if that horrible feeling ever went away, she'd quit on the spot.

It didn't appear Rebecca would be able to quit anytime soon. In fact, she could use some stomach medicine about now. And a coffee.

The techs had already pulled the blankets out of the van. Inspected, swabbed, and neatly folded away into bags, they told the story she'd thought they would. Purple chalk was smeared on one side of the blanket, orange on the other. Rebecca guessed the girl had tucked the orange chalk somewhere against her body before she was taken. She closed her eyes, imagining the child setting the purple chalk down on the sidewalk to pet the golden-haired puppy that had left its fur on the other blanket.

Along with the second piece of chalk, the orange one, they'd found long, brown hairs and several blond strands as well. These blankets could have been used to transport at least two of the girls, if not all three. They would have to DNA test them and the blue hat to be certain.

They'd already linked Sylvie and a puppy to this van. If they could connect a person with the puppy, they would have a solid suspect. It wasn't as good as spotting Sylvie in the video, but it would help.

Rebecca's phone pinged with a message from Hoyt. *Good news.*

What followed was good news indeed.

Screengrabs of the two vehicles connected to the van along with a name. Tammy Carr.

Another text came through. *Married to Jon Carr. Adding all info to the case file.*

Hope wanted to fill Rebecca's chest, but she forced it down. She'd allow herself to feel something besides urgency when Sylvie Harper was safe and sound.

After sending a *Good job* text back to Hoyt, she sprinted to the cruiser and pulled out the laptop to connect to the file. As she watched the screen, new files came in.

She tapped out a text to Hoyt, asking him to look into any locals who might have sold, or were missing, a puppy with tan or golden fur. She also let him know to check the case file online. There was more than enough evidence now to update the Amber Alert.

Using the hood of the cruiser as a desk, Rebecca typed in the vehicle information for the Altima and the Intrepid. She also put out an APB to cover all their bases. As she did that, she realized the radio had been surprisingly quiet for awhile.

Then again, with Hoyt and Greg at the station with Viviane, Trent working the traffic stops, and Darian here with her, there was no need for radio chatter. Having texted an update to Hoyt, the radio could remain silent, allowing the techs to focus on their tasks.

"Here you go." Darian handed her an SD card. "This one's full."

Rebecca had asked the young deputy to take pictures of all the evidence before it was bagged so everyone else could follow their progress.

"Thanks." She then gave him a brief update on Hoyt's findings.

With a renewed gleam in his eyes, Darian snapped a second SD card into the camera. "We'll find those girls." Before she could respond, he walked away to finish his project.

Another car pulled up near the entrance to the tiny parking area. Rebecca kept part of her attention on the new arrival while sorting through the pictures and tagging the ones she wanted Hoyt to pay attention to. They needed to keep an eye out for any further smudges of chalk anywhere too. That was a detail she'd made sure Darian got excellent pictures of.

As she worked, Rebecca watched the driver get out of the vehicle. He was clearly a Fed of some flavor. She observed as he made a production of pulling on his thin FBI-issued jacket before heading her way. He ducked under the crime scene tape, walked past her, and presented himself in front of Darian with fists on hips.

She rolled her eyes so hard she thought she'd strained something. But Darian was a good man. He could take care of himself.

"Do I look like a sheriff?" Darian's voice rang out, chock-full of disbelief and sarcasm. "If you look real close, you can see the word *Deputy* right here. I know it's real shiny, and the dipping sun might be in your eyes, but you should still be able to read it."

"Hudson," Rebecca called out without turning away from her current task.

"Yes, ma'am." His voice dripped with respect for her.

Had all cops hated me as instantly as Darian seems to hate this guy?

She smiled. Probably. The Feds tried to work with the locals, but it was sometimes like mixing oil and water.

She glanced at the time and looked at Darian. "That mold should be ready by now. Can you check with the techs? I'd like to get those loaded up as quickly as possible."

"Yes, ma'am." There was a slide of shoes on sand, then a pause. "As you heard, that's our sheriff. Watch where you put your feet. This is an active crime scene."

Ah, rookies. The favorite snack of all law enforcement officers.

If she had the time or patience for it, she'd join in and set his tail on fire as well. It was a good thing for him she didn't have any to spare.

The suit appeared by her side. "I'm Agent Christopher Stalwart—"

"I'm not going to take your word for it. Whip it out and show me."

"E-excuse me?"

Oh damn, she hadn't been able to help herself after all. Rebecca unclipped her badge from her belt and wiggled it in his face while she typed one-handed. "I show you mine. And now you show me yours. What did you think I meant?"

The kid started patting his pockets for his ID. "You're the sheriff?" He stopped patting and stared at her, leaning in too close for comfort.

Rebecca hooked her badge back onto her pants. Closing her eyes, she took a deep breath and let it out slowly. In all fairness, she wasn't wearing a uniform, but still... "Deputy Hudson! Remove this unidentified man from my crime scene."

"Yes, ma'am!" There was a shuffle of feet as Darian happily made his way over to them. Even the techs were standing up and paying attention now, everyone instantly on edge.

"I've got it right here. Right here." Agent Stalwart finally pulled his credentials out of his pocket and flashed the wallet open.

Rebecca turned and inspected the ID. "Stand down, Hudson. He's just slow, not a criminal."

Darian let out a disappointed sigh and turned back to the scene, making the techs laugh as they got back to work.

"I understand you're new to crime scenes, Agent Stalwart. Data analysts don't often come out in the field. But do remember that you need to have your credentials ready before you step under the tape next time." She smiled to soften the criticism. "Now, what do you need?"

One of the techs alerted her. "Mold's ready, Sheriff."

Rebecca opened a new window and was ready to type. "Any unique features?"

"Nothing in this strip. The tires aren't new. Tread's a little worn, but nothing to catch the attention. No knicks or cuts. No residue discernable. We'll check the sand later. But it does jive with the tan Nissan Altima you saw in the footage. That's about all I can tell you right now."

"Nothing on the Intrepid?"

He shook his head. "Not yet."

"It was a long shot, but always worth checking. Thanks. Agent Stalwart, I can do two things at once. Can you at least do one?"

"What? Oh, sorry. Um…"

"What do you need, Agent?"

"I was sent down to take over your investigation."

Her fingers didn't pause in her typing. "This is a bad time for jokes, Stalwart."

"Jokes? But…"

It suddenly clicked. "Did Benson send you down here?"

"Special Agent in Charge Benson? Yes, uh, ma'am, he did. Why do you ask?"

"He's hazing you, Stalwart. He sent you here to get your nose twisted, and normally, I'd love to do that. I had a reputation for doing just that back when I was a special agent, which is probably why Benson sent you to me. But right now, there are three little girls about to be sold into sexual slavery, so how about we put all the nut-busting aside and get back to our jobs. Okay? I'll call and rip Benson a new one later."

Rebecca made a mental note to send Benson a glitter-filled card as soon as she could. They'd had a prank war going for years now, and while he often said she took things too far, he always had crappy timing.

"Ma'am…um, Sheriff, I—"

"I could tear apart your rookie mistakes for the next hour and figure out what you've done to get sent to work with me, but here's the abridged version. You didn't do your due diligence. That's not a good trait in an analyst, especially one who works in the field and doesn't have a lot of experience."

She finished her update and turned to face the man.

"Well, I—"

"You should have known as soon as Benson told you to take over our case that that isn't what you do. FBI show up to offer support."

Stalwart stared at her with his jaw hanging open. "I—"

"Taking over slows down the investigation and creates friction between agencies. A slowed kidnapping investigation leads to more bodies later. Second, my name and picture are attached to the file as lead investigator and sheriff. You'd have known that if you'd read the file completely. You looked like an incompetent fool, walking in here without identifying yourself and tromping all over a crime scene with techs, and you didn't even address them or ask if it was clear to walk where you did. Thankfully, the rest of us were paying attention and didn't allow you to screw up anything important. Just your reputation."

"I—"

"Now, you have one chance to redeem yourself. It's possible that I've got one, possibly two, people trying to move three girls out of this area. Most likely for sale to a pre-established buyer, considering our main suspect has done this before, and those girls have never been found. I've got Coast Guard running a blockade and a checkpoint on the only road out of here." She pointed to the ocean that was somewhere to the east.

He raised a hand. "How—"

"You need to get me a list of known traffickers and cache points in the area we've established in the case files, plus a seven-hour drive or boat ride in each direction. Then you need to figure out how long we have before the three children we're trying to save vanish forever."

Rebecca stopped to give the man a look, indicating he should be taking notes.

And like that, the agent whipped out a notebook.

"I also need all the information you can dig up on Jon—J-O-N no H, Carr, two Rs—and Tammy with a Y, same last name. I need to know their residences for the last seven years. Any place they've rented. Any place they've paid utilities. Any pets they might own. And any family or known acquaintances. Think you can do all that?"

Agent Stalwart gulped hard enough to swallow his tongue and nodded. "Y-es, ma...Sheriff."

"Ma'am is fine. So is sir. Or Sheriff. But we're running out of daylight, so get a move on."

"Yes, ma'am." Stalwart shuffled away, heading back to his car.

"I found gold!"

Rebecca spun around.

A forensic tech was walking around the driver's side of the van toward her and holding up a fingerprint tape.

"Tell me you got a print." Rebecca prayed as she approached him.

"I sure did. A good one, too, probably from his thumb. It was on the back of the seat belt catch, which had fallen between the seats and was missed in the wipe down."

"Now please tell me you've got a fingerprint reader on you." Rebecca smiled hopefully.

"The lady is winning all the big prizes today. Just follow me to my bag of tricks."

Rebecca followed him over, joined shortly by Darian, as the tech flipped the sealed tape over the reader. A beep followed an agonizing number of seconds later.

"Jon, no *H*, Carr, two *Rs*." He grinned and turned the reader around so they could both read the screen. It was Jon Carr's mugshot. "You've got your man, all right."

"We will soon." Darian headed over to the laptop. "I'll update the Amber Alert and everything else."

Rebecca held up a hand. "I'll do that. I need to ask Chincoteague PD to raid his house. It's still his listed residence, after all. If he left the island right after we saw him here, he could be there by now. If he's not, it'll be one less secure place he can take them."

Rebecca made it back to the car at the same time Stalwart wandered back, carrying his tablet.

"And Agent Stalwart…"

He turned to face her.

She tried to offer him a reassuring smile after ripping him to shreds just minutes ago. "You'll forgive me for earlier. We're in the thick of it here, and stress is replacing patience. You didn't screw up anything."

His face relaxed. "Thank you, ma'am."

She smiled. "At least you were smart enough to come to the secondary crime scene instead of doing something stupid, like going to the sheriff's office first."

18

Sylvie hugged her knees to her chest and stared at the screen in front of her. Her bottom and legs still burned from where the bad man had hit her with the book, but she refused to rub the sore spots. And she refused to cry.

When she'd first woken up, she'd been confused about where she was. She still wasn't sure, but she knew it wasn't home. It wasn't even that nice place she'd been staying at, near the beach.

Maybe she wasn't even at the beach anymore. Sylvie couldn't smell the pretty ocean air. What she did smell, she didn't want to think about. And no matter how hard she thought, she couldn't remember how she'd gotten here. It was like those times she would fall asleep on the couch or at the table and would wake up in her own bed.

Had she fallen asleep and didn't remember it?

The last thing she did remember was petting a puppy. Dad had been singing, and she went outside to draw on the sidewalk. Then a puppy walked up to her. She thought she remembered how its fur felt under her hands, and maybe it was scared. Or hurt?

She couldn't remember.

It almost felt like trying to remember a dream. Maybe it had all been a dream. But there was a little bit of orange and purple chalk smudged in the creases on her palms.

So that part was real.

Was the puppy? Where was he? She hoped he was doing better than she was.

Her head hurt, her mouth tasted funny, and her belly kept making noises. And she wasn't alone.

There were two other girls in the room. They didn't talk much, not even when she'd asked their names. But they had joined her when she'd started crying that she wanted a snack. Dad said she could always ask for a snack. She was a growing girl and needed to eat when she was hungry, so she would get big and strong. There were always carrots and radishes in the fridge for her to grab. Or crackers in the pantry where she could reach them.

No one had answered when she'd first called out, so she'd gotten louder, thinking whoever was babysitting just hadn't heard. She didn't know why someone would be babysitting while she was on vacation, or who the other girls were, but it was the only thing that made sense. Her parents didn't leave her alone without a babysitter. Maybe she'd fallen asleep, and her parents went to the beach and left her with a babysitter. If they had, he was a really scary one.

She'd called and called and called, asking for food. When that hadn't worked, she'd called for her momma. Thinking they still couldn't hear her, she'd called out through the crack under the door, hoping someone would hear her and get one of her parents. That hadn't ended so good. She'd hurt her face when something had struck the door.

She really didn't like it here.

Neither of the other girls had said a word since that man had spanked her.

They'd gone back to their spots in the room and just sat there. But then, there wasn't really anything else to do. The room they were stuck in was smelly and dirty, and there was no furniture. There were mattresses, but they were all stuck to the walls. A little bit of light came in from behind one of the mattresses, but the only other light came from the weird cube-shaped screen in front of her. It was a TV, but it didn't look like any television she'd ever seen. It was too fat and not very wide. Also, it sat on the floor instead of hanging on a wall.

There was some kind of box or something underneath it. It looked kinda like her momma's internet cube but was much bigger. Also, it didn't show the connection lights, just a flashing twelve o'clock, no matter how many times she tapped on the tiny screen. Momma had always said she was a natural with computers, but Sylvie couldn't get this one to work at all.

It didn't even have a reset button. There was a large flap on one side that flipped in when she pressed on it, and she could feel the computer whirring in there, but she couldn't get it to do anything. Not even go to a home screen. She kept tapping and swiping in both directions, hoping something would come up. If she could find a messaging app, maybe she could find a way to contact Momma or Dad.

Maybe it was broken or locked. She poked it again, this time harder, and the big cube of a screen on top of it wobbled a bit.

"Be careful," the blond girl hissed. "If we make too much noise, he'll come in and hurt us."

"I want my mommy." The other girl, the one with the short, dark, curly hair, whimpered.

"I want my momma too." Sylvie's eyes burned. "Do you think he was right? Do you think Momma won't want me anymore because I broke the rules and left the yard? I know I wasn't supposed to."

"My mommy would love me no matter what I did." Curly haired girl leaned forward. "I bet your mommy loves you just as much too."

That made Sylvie feel a little bit better.

"My mommy always said she loves me more than coffee. And that's a lot." The yellow-haired girl giggled. There was something wrong with her smile, though. It looked broken and like it didn't have a lot of happy in it. Smiles were always supposed to look happy. Her eyes were funny too. And the skin under them was pulled in, making them bug out a little bit. It was almost like she was sick, but she wasn't coughing or sneezing.

Sylvie didn't want to say anything because both girls looked so sad already, but they also smelled really bad. Or maybe it was just the room they were in. When she'd first had to potty, both girls had pointed to a bucket in the corner. Unsure why, she'd made the mistake of walking over and looking inside. It was full of dookie and peepee.

She'd run away from it as quickly as she could and decided she didn't need to potty as badly as she thought. Besides, if she peed, then she'd need to take off her swimsuit, and she didn't want the other girls to see her that way.

Since then, she'd stayed as far away from the bucket as she could, along with the others. They were all huddled against the wall, each on their own. The other two were fixated on the cartoon playing on the screen. Sylvie didn't recognize it, but then, she wasn't allowed a lot of screen time.

She wanted to go home. She wanted to use a bathroom. She wanted to go make sandcastles on the beach with her dad and listen to him sing his silly song about cheeseburgers again.

Did all of this happen because she was a bad girl?

Remembering what Momma had told her, Sylvie crawled over to one of the blankets. It was the closest thing she had to a bed. She sat on her knees, tucking her feet under her butt, and pressed her palms together in front of her face. Closing her eyes, she bowed her head, touching her thumbs to her lips.

"Our Father, who art in Heaven, hello to your name. I'm really sorry I was a bad girl. I promise I won't ever leave the yard again unless Momma and Dad tell me it's okay. I promise I won't try to go play without them either. Please tell Momma and Dad I'm really sorry and ask them to come get me, please. Thank you, amen."

Sylvie lifted her head and waited.

The two girls stared at her. Their eyes were wide and looked even sadder now. She wasn't sure why. Was it because they didn't know how to pray?

Before Sylvie could ask them, she heard a noise.

It came from outside the room. Sylvie crawled over to the door, pressing her ear against the crack at the bottom. Two men were talking out there. She couldn't tell what they were saying, but it was definitely two voices talking.

Probably the big man who'd dangled her in the air.

But...what if her dad was out there? She had to try.

Twisting her head around, Sylvie pressed her cheek against the ground. "Dad, is that you? I'm in here, Dad. I'm sorry I was bad. Can I have a snack, please? My belly is making noises."

Not wanting the door to hit her again, Sylvie jerked up and scooted away from it to wait.

There was silence for a minute, then footsteps coming closer. There was a laugh she didn't recognize. Then the weird lock without a doorknob clicked.

Sylvie jumped to her feet, ready to fling herself into her dad's arms and tell him how sorry she was.

The door opened, and the big man with big arms stood there, staring down at her. He looked so angry. Sylvie backed away. He had one arm tucked behind his back.

"You girls are hungry?"

Sylvie looked at the others. When they didn't respond, she just nodded. If he gave her something to eat, she would share it with them. Snacks always tasted better when you had someone to share them with. "Y-es."

The big man smiled at her. There was happy in it, but it still scared her. "Then it's time you learned a lesson."

Sylvie didn't like the sound of that and started scooting farther away.

"Eat," the big man's arm came out from behind his back, "or be eaten."

Before Sylvie could react or even scream, he flung a rat in her face.

19

Rebecca walked back into the station, leading Deputy Hudson and Agent Stalwart. The forensic techs had gotten them as much information as they could in the field. The tow truck had shown up, and they'd carted the van off to the evidence locker to go over in a more professional setting.

As soon as they'd gotten Jon's mugshot, Rebecca had updated the Amber Alert with him as a possible person of interest. APBs had been sent to every law enforcement station in all of Virginia and its neighboring states.

There had been what looked like a child's fingerprint on the floor trim of the sliding door, but it had been so small and delicate, the techs didn't want to risk pulling it with their field kits. After being assured she would be continuously updated as they gathered more information, Rebecca had left the scene. She'd done all she could there, and she was easier to reach at the station.

The Amber Alert sounded on her phone as she drove, and she felt a sense of accomplishment at having gotten it out so fast. It had been less than eight hours since they'd gotten the first call, and they already had solid leads and a suspect with priors. She wasn't one to rest on her laurels, though, so as soon as they walked into the station, she started handing out new marching orders.

"Hudson, check the APB. Stalwart, use the office in back. Viviane, can you order us some pizzas or anything we can eat while working?" A woman with light brown hair stood up from one of the rows of seats in the lobby, catching Rebecca's attention. It took Rebecca a moment to place her, but then she realized she'd been at the ceremony. Angie Frost. She once again had a package in her hands. "Frost, did you know your wife is here?"

"I might be on light duty, but I'm not blind." His response, which carried from the bullpen, was tailed by an amused chuckle.

"Actually, Sheriff, I'm here for you." Mrs. Frost stepped forward, lifting a plastic bag. "Darian called his wife. She didn't know what to do, so she called me. She said you needed some uniform parts, but there wasn't anything in your size here at the station, so I dug through my closet and got this for you."

"Uniform?" Rebecca opened the bag and saw a thick leather belt. It wasn't standard issue, but it was black and had a few pouches on it.

"No uniform, I'm afraid, but I managed to cobble a duty belt from Hoyt's spare tools and the widest belt I owned. I wasn't sure if there was a specific order they should go in, but I did my best to put it all together."

"Can't have the sheriff losing her britches at the crime scene." Viviane smiled at them, a twinkle in her eye.

"Or her radio." Darian moved over to his desk. "Like I said, Boss. Civvy clothes just aren't up to the rigors of this job."

Pulling the belt from the bag, Rebecca saw that it was a bit wider than a standard woman's belt. A set of handcuffs, a mini flashlight, a clip for her radio, a pouch for gloves, and another for handcuff keys. A second set of cuffs was in their leather case. Even with the duty belt out, the bag was heavy. She peeked inside to see what else it contained.

"Those are spare mags. I wasn't sure what you carried or if his holster would fit your gun, but I brought them just in case."

Rebecca was deeply touched by the kind gesture from everyone. She realized the smile on her face was the first she'd worn all day. "I don't carry a Glock, but it's very kind of you to think of this."

"Oh, then you won't need those." Mrs. Frost took the bag back. "I'll take them with me. I just wanted to make sure you had as much of everything that you needed. Darian asked his wife to have her mother bring up one of his spare belts, but we knew that wouldn't fit you. No offense to him, but belts can only cinch so far, you know?"

Rebecca smiled at the tickle of laughter coming from Mrs. Frost. "This is amazing. Thank you so much."

"We did the best we could. I hope that will suit you 'til you can get a new one ordered."

"Mrs. Frost, I don't know what to say—"

"Please, call me Angie. Let's keep the formal titles to the boys, shall we?"

Rebecca smiled at that. The "boys" were all older than her. Well, except Darian. He was a few years younger but having a newborn in the house made it hard to tell, with the bags under his eyes. She hoped she'd be able to send him home soon to spend more time with his new family.

"Angie, thank you so much. You don't know how touching this is." Unable to hold herself back, Rebecca leaned in and placed a kiss on Angie's cheek. She almost regretted the emotional outburst, but Angie's motherly smile wiped that away instantly.

"Hey, I want some of that action too."

Angie and Rebecca both pulled back and stared at Hoyt as he stepped into the lobby, but he only had eyes for his wife. He wrapped both arms around her shoulders and pulled her in to plant a kiss on her forehead.

"My wife is the best. A kind heart, a thoughtful soul, and a hell of a cook." For a heartbeat, the Frosts were transformed, gazing into each other's eyes. The years of love and companionship were obvious to everyone.

Viviane gave a sappy little sigh, and Rebecca ducked her head to put her new belt on. By the time she was done cinching it into place and moving everything just where she wanted, the couple had pulled back a little, at least far enough that they wouldn't inflict spontaneous cavities on anyone who laid eyes on them.

"Fits like a glove." Rebecca twisted side to side, showing off her much-needed accessory.

"Speaking of gloves, you're going to want to swap those out." Hoyt waved his long fingers. "Mine will be way too big for you."

"And floppy gloves are the worst." Angie offered a knowing nod.

"Also, Sheriff, I found a post for a lost puppy on Instagram. Golden retriever, nine weeks old. Goes by the name Nugget. Went missing last night, still hasn't been found. His owner, a thirteen-year-old boy, is heartbroken, according to the mom. I gotta admit, the pup looks irresistible with those big, fluffy ears."

"A lost dog?" His wife swatted at him gently. "Don't you think the sheriff has more pressing matters to attend to?"

"Actually, this could be relevant to our case. Can you follow up on that, Frost? See if they had Nugget chipped. Or if he has one of those GPS trackers on his collar. The more links we have, the tighter the case will be."

"I sure will. Looks like it's just a couple blocks away, so I'll just walk over."

"But don't let them know why we're asking, at least not in front of the boy." Rebecca headed back to the bullpen. "And check to see if they recognize the van too. And check for CCTV nearby. If our perps lured the pup, we might catch them in the act and spot anything new that could be helpful."

"Yeah, Boss, will do." Hoyt planted another kiss on his wife's forehead. "Honey, I love you. I'll see you tonight as soon as I can."

Angie patted his stomach. "How about I drop you off, so you'll only have to walk back?"

Hoyt headed toward the door. "Sounds like a plan."

Angie made it to the exit before stopping. "Rebecca, it was good to see you again. Good luck with your investigation."

"Thanks again, Angie."

"Bye!" Angie waved and disappeared through the door.

Rebecca detoured toward the coffeepot when Greg, sitting at his desk, stopped her. "Got anything for me, Sheriff?" He threw his hands out, as if waiting for her to toss him some work.

"Yeah, can you call Meg, the volunteers, and the search party? Let them all know we're looking for traces of orange and purple chalk as well. And a golden retriever puppy."

Greg frowned, and every wrinkle in his sixty-one-year-old face sank deeper into his deeply tanned skin. "We're following up on a puppy?"

"We're following every lead we get." Rebecca searched his expression for any hint of criticism and found none.

"How big's the pup?"

"Nine-week-old golden retriever." Rebecca shrugged, holding her hands out in front of her. "He'd be about this big."

"Puppy that young would need to be walked fairly often too." He tapped his temple. "And draws lots of attention."

Darian handed Rebecca the cup of coffee she hadn't managed to reach yet. "You got something, Greg?"

"Something. Yeah, but I can't remember who said it. Lemme go ask some people." Greg hoisted himself out of his chair and headed for the door. "You can use my desk, Sheriff. Best to keep that Feebie kid in back, where he can't piss anyone off."

Rebecca sipped at the hot elixir of life, wondering how Agent Stalwart could have possibly pissed on anyone here. *Maybe he did come to the station before reporting to the scene?*

"That's his thinking face." Darian nodded at Greg's back. "He's remembered something but wants to verify the source before he lets us know. Old school."

She shrugged. "What about the APB?"

Darian shook his head. "No hits, but Chincoteague PD and state SWAT are about to hit the Carr residence. Warrant came in a few minutes ago."

"Wish I could be there." Rebecca sat down in Greg's empty seat.

"You and everyone else involved. This sitting around is the worst part of the job." Darian sat too, poking his mouse to clear the screen saver that had just popped up. "But they're an hour away, and no reason for them to wait around for us." The deputy chewed on his lip for a moment before turning to look at her again. "You think Tammy Carr might still be on the island?"

"I do." Rebecca signed into the sheriff's account on Greg's computer. "We got things locked down pretty quick, and we can only hope the kidnappers are moving slow and careful after the grab. Switching cars and scheduling meetups take time. Also, I have to believe it."

"You have to? Why?"

Rebecca kept her eyes on her screen, refusing to look at the new father. "Because if they got Sylvie off the island, then she's gone. Really gone. If they were in a hurry to move, then it's most likely because they had a drop-off scheduled. Once that happens, it's almost impossible to trace them."

"What will they do with her?" Darian's voice was barely above a whisper.

"They'll keep changing hands, shuffling the kids around, splitting them up, joining different groups, giving them different names each time until they're lost. If that happens, we're looking for needles in needlestacks. There's a reason the FBI has a fully staffed task force searching for these cretins at all times. Because they're always moving, always working, and they don't stop unless we make them."

"Then we make them stop." Darian's voice was still low, but the earnestness made her want to hug him.

She looked over at Wallace's plaque, wondering for the briefest moment how he'd have handled the day. What would his first move have been?

Wait...Wallace.

She closed her eyes, watching her thoughts play out in her mind before voicing them. "I'd bet big money that these professionals were planning to move the girls off-island at a time when local law enforcement was distracted. Like during the sheriff's funeral."

Darian's nostrils flared. "I bet you're right. And if you are, it more solidly means they're still here."

Rebecca glanced over at him, at the hope in his eyes, and immediately rethought his age. He couldn't be more than thirty and still have that kind of hope and optimism in his heart, not in this line of work.

Or maybe she was the one who'd lost her hope and optimism too soon.

Blood on the linoleum.

Screaming.
Blood on the cupboards.
Her mother's limp hands in hers.
The coldness.
Covered in blood.

Rebecca shook her head and blew out a heavy breath. This was no time to give in to the nightmares. Especially since she was fully awake.

A notification popped up on her screen, and she was saved from having to say something that would steal the hope from the deputy's eyes.

"SWAT's moving in. I asked them to set up a live stream so we could get an answer on Sylvie as soon as possible."

Darian rolled over to her. Viviane jumped out of her chair. She took a few steps, then froze.

Understanding her indecision, Rebecca shook her head, letting Viviane know she didn't want to see what was about to occur on the screen.

"I'll let you know what happens."

Viviane nodded and moved back to her seat.

On the screen, the officer with the live body camera was crouched behind his fellow officer. There was no sound because they weren't looped into the audio. For a few minutes, nothing happened as everyone moved into position.

They would be breaching with a no-knock warrant, not allowing the Carrs to escape or get to the girls, if possible.

With no audio to give her a clue on the timing, Rebecca jumped a little when the officer began to move, his camera bouncing with each hurried step. It was a chaotic mess of jumbling shapes, snippets of a room, then a doorway, then another room.

The officer jerked to the side, and his weapon blocked part of the frame. A wall. A bed. A closet. The same bed again. A closet door was swung open as they raced forward, then stopped. A crazed blur of what appeared to be men's clothing was shoved aside.

It was similar to being there in person, except for the silence. A spin, another doorway, then the sight of a bullet-proof vest with SWAT emblazoned across the front of it. The two teams had met in the middle after coming in from the front and back doors simultaneously.

Rebecca knew what was happening, even though she couldn't hear it. Different voices were calling out that each room was clear. If they'd found anyone, they would have rushed to that point instead of milling around, letting their adrenaline seep away. The bodies were crowded and still shuffling around, but much slower this time.

Blood on linoleum.

Rebecca breathed out in a long exhale, reminding herself she was at the station watching and not actually on scene. She didn't need to hold her breath or breathe shallowly to keep her gun steady. Which was good, since her hands were shaking.

Out in the field, she was fine. She knew what she was doing. She knew where she was. But watching it...

It's like I'm there again. Watching myself moving as if it were a movie. I'm not in charge. I'm just along for the ride as someone else finds my mother's body in the kitchen, lying in a puddle of her blood. Someone else is screaming in my voice. Someone else is crying out for my mom. My dad. It's not me, it's—

"It's empty." Darian jolted her out of her memory.

Rebecca straightened her shoulders, hiding how deflated she felt. "Yeah, looks like no one has been there for awhile. There was dust on the coffee table." She was proud of herself for noticing that. It had only been on the screen for a second, but the gray haze on the cherry wood had stood out. "But there are men's clothes in the bedroom with a woman's robe hanging on the door. Either Tammy has a live-in boyfriend, or she and her husband aren't as separated as they claim."

"Or vice versa. She could have moved out, and he moved in."

"True. We'll find out soon enough." Rebecca picked up her cup, willing her hand to steady before taking a sip. "With the vehicle swapping, I didn't think we'd find the girls at the Carr residence, but it would have been nice."

Closing the window, she looked up at Viviane. She looked like she'd been watching them the entire time. Rebecca hoped the fear Viviane must have seen on her face could be explained away by what they were watching. She shook her head. "No one was there."

Viviane sank into her chair, disappointment and worry taking claim on her face. "We'll get them. Don't worry."

"Ya know, seems weird to me that a wife, one who says she doesn't live with her husband because she can't get past their history together, would still be married to a man accused of kidnapping three girls. Especially after they lost a child. What kind of parent could inflict that type of pain on another parent when they already know how it feels?"

Rebecca had thought the same thing. "You think she was involved in the first case too?"

Darian pinned her with his pale brown eyes. "Don't you?"

"I'd bet money on it, but I've got a more disturbing question."

It was Darian's turn to frown. "What's that?"

"What happened to their baby? Was it a boy? Or a girl?"

"I can dig that up for you," Viviane offered. "Oh, hold on. Frost's calling in." She reached up and tapped the headpiece hidden by her hair. "Frost, what you got for us?"

Darian and Rebecca both watched as she nodded with an "uh-huh" a few times.

"Okay, see you in a bit." Viviane's cheeks puffed as she blew out a breath. "Frost said the puppy is still missing, and the mom thinks she saw the van in her neighborhood when she took the puppy for his nighttime walk. She also said the neighbors across the street got a new video doorbell, and he should ask them for the video. They have the neighbor's work number, so they're calling to see if they can get that to us as soon as possible. The boy wasn't there because he's still out looking for Nugget."

Poor kid.

"Does anyone know if a warrant was pulled for Tammy's bank records yet?" Rebecca turned back to her computer. "If not, we need to get one. If so, we need to get our hands on them. See if she bought anything local. Like dog biscuits, or gas, or anything. See if she's been in Lynnhaven or Sandbridge."

She was reaching, she knew. It wasn't likely that a professional would be lax enough to use a credit card or ATM in the town where they were committing crimes, but criminals often did stupid things. Like using their personal vehicles to haul kidnapped children around.

Maybe they'd gotten so confident they didn't worry about playing it too safe.

"We know who we're looking for now, but we need to know where they are. Where they've been can tell us where they're going next."

"I know a judge who'll get us that warrant." Darian shook his computer mouse to clear the screen saver again.

"Do it."

Darian turned to his screen and froze. "Maybe we don't need to."

Rebecca checked her computer and saw a new notification. She refreshed the page.

"They've got a hit on the tan Altima. It's parked outside a

bar in Sandbridge." Darian read it out as she skimmed over the notice.

Rebecca took over reading. "Officers on scene have eyes on Tammy. No sign of Jon yet, so they're still looking." She stood up, checking her pockets for the cruiser keys.

"I've got 'em. I know where the bar is too." Darian jingled the keys at her as he pushed his chair back.

"Let's run this hot and loud. If Jon's still here, he'll hear us leaving. Might make him come out of whatever hole he's hiding in. And everyone is looking for him now that we've added his face to the Amber Alert." Rebecca pushed away from her borrowed desk, and Darian fell in behind her as they headed for the parking lot.

"Viviane, call Deputy Locke and tell him to make a hole for us."

20

Knuckles white, Rebecca kept herself braced against the passenger door as Deputy Hudson wove through the island's light traffic and hit the bridge doing sixty-five miles per hour. Cars moved to either side, allowing them a straight shot through, so they didn't even need to slow down.

She caught Trent's face for just a moment. He was scowling but gave them a half-hearted salute as they whipped past. The sun would be setting soon, and the siren echoed across the water, letting everyone know they were coming.

Rebecca gritted her teeth, not because of Darian's fine handling of the speeding cruiser or how closely he slid between bumpers. What bothered her was the idea that the kidnappers might panic and act in a destructive way. She'd been the one to tell Darian to run it loud, letting everyone on the island know the cops were leaving.

The hope had been that it would make them feel free to move from wherever they were hiding. But there was no telling if they would leave their merchandise behind, dispose of it, or try to take it with them. She'd bet on the kidnappers being professional and not wanting to lose out on their money.

A lot was riding on her being right. She hoped she hadn't screwed everything up. Hoyt, Trent, and Greg were still on the island. And most of the town already knew about the missing children thanks to the flyers and alerts.

All she could do was hope.

Ten minutes after leaving the station, Darian pulled up in front of a tiki bar, sliding in between several other cop cars. There were even two CSI trucks parked, with the forensic techs milling around, waiting on someone to give directions. A few heads popped up at their arrival, mostly uniformed officers, one of whom walked over to check them.

"Sheriff West from Shadow Island. I hear you guys have eyes on our suspect."

The officer glanced at the badge she held, then over to Darian, who gave the nod that every cop seemed to have.

Hail, fellow, well met.

"Yes, ma'am, a Tammy Carr. Her vehicle is in the lot, but we haven't touched it yet. Officer Brown is inside, talking with her. He's in charge."

That last part was said as if the uniform wasn't certain of who was in charge now. It was fine with Rebecca. She wasn't going to get into a pissing match about territory. This was her suspect but not her jurisdiction. So long as she got answers, that was all she cared about.

"Can you get your forensic team down here? And have you checked the vehicle for passengers?"

"Passengers, ma'am? No one is in the car."

"Did you check the trunk? We do know a puppy was placed in her trunk." Rebecca's stomach tightened. "Make sure it's no longer there."

The uniform looked over at the other officers waiting

around. When none of them nodded, he shook his head. "I don't know, ma'am. I just arrived on scene."

Rebecca arched one eyebrow. "Can you check?"

"Yeah, I'll do that now." He turned and moved off, not quite running.

Not willing to waste anymore time, Rebecca turned and headed into the bar. It was clear where she needed to go, as there was a small huddle of uniforms around a booth. A tall man with a white towel draped over his shoulder chatted with another uniformed officer off to the side.

In the booth was a bleached-blond woman who appeared to be in her early fifties wearing an off-the-shoulder blouse. She was crying.

Tammy Carr.

Rebecca frowned as she noticed that, despite the confused look on the woman's face and the tears running down her cheeks, her makeup wasn't smudged, and her eyes weren't red. They were wide and pleading as she spoke to an officer holding a pair of handcuffs.

The officer ignored whatever she was saying and helped her to her feet. Tammy didn't resist as he turned her around and clamped the cuffs around her wrists.

Rebecca moved closer, wanting to know what the woman was saying.

"You don't understand...I can't divorce him without permission from the church."

That explained how she'd kept her name off the report the last time. The woman was a brilliant actress.

Tammy was mid-spiel, so Rebecca walked right past her. No reason to stop her now. Best to let her keep pouring out whatever story she was spinning, so Rebecca could use it against her later.

Approaching the man who had to be the bartender, she nodded to the officer he was speaking to.

"Sheriff West?"

"That's me."

"If you don't mind, I'd rather hand this all over to you." He tipped his head to where Tammy was still making a case for freedom. "We don't have anything to charge her with. She's a person of interest in your case."

"The plates match the APB?"

"Plates match. Same make and model, but she swears she's been here all day."

"Are there any cameras?"

"Just the ones in the lots. Front and back. None inside."

Rebecca turned to the bartender. "Has she been here all day?"

"Well, she's been here since we opened. But after two drinks, she did leave to get something to eat, according to her. Came back after that to have a few more drinks and hang out. She even gave me her keys to prove she wasn't going anywhere."

"Do you still have those on you?" This was a serious break in the case. And there was nothing saying the woman didn't have two sets of keys for her car.

"Yeah, behind the bar. Do you want—"

"As quickly as you can, please. We need to see if there's anything important in the vehicle."

Like a child or a puppy.

The bartender made his way behind the bar, and they followed him over. "This is all about those missing kids? I can't believe Tammy would have anything to do with that." He started digging around.

"What makes you think that?"

"Well, we saw it on the news, and a couple locals were talking about it. She piped up, saying her husband had once been accused of taking kids previously too. Said it had all turned out to be nothing. Except it had ruined his reputation.

I thought it was just a way for her to get free drinks. People like buying drinks for someone telling stories, ya know? Except she got real teary-eyed about it, explaining how awful it was to deal with, and kept tossing back the liquor."

He handed over the keys to Rebecca along with a credit card. "She was holding open a tab. I guess I should give this to you too."

Rebecca nodded and passed both items to Darian. He headed out, signaling one of the Sandbridge officers to join him.

"Did she say anything else about that old case?"

"Just that she should've divorced her husband back then but didn't want to kick him while he was down. And they've been separated since then."

Since then, eh? Not what she'd told the newspaper years back. Rebecca wondered how often her story changed.

"Thought she said it turned out to be nothing."

He nodded. "That's what she said."

"Then why leave him?"

Confusion crossed the bartender's expression like a wave. He opened his mouth and closed it again. "Are you allowed to just search her car like that?"

Nice change of subject.

"That vehicle was used in a crime earlier today, so yes. It's evidence in an ongoing investigation, and we can take possession. The warrant has already been filed."

"Oh. Okay. I just don't want to get in trouble and lose my job for giving away a customer's belongings."

Officer Brown patted the bartender on the shoulder. "No trouble at all. You're cooperating with the police. If your boss gives you any hassle about any of this, just give us a call." He handed over a business card.

"Will do. Is that all, Officers? I've got a job to get back to. These barflies won't water themselves."

Officer Brown glanced over to check with Rebecca, but she was already speaking. "Can we get the footage from your security cameras?"

The bartender reached under the bar and pulled out a thumb drive. "I got it ready when the first cops showed up. Figured you'd want it."

She smiled. "A good bartender knows what customers want."

"And cops always want evidence." He grinned at her, then walked off to help the man flagging him down at the other end of the bar.

Even with all the cops showing up, it didn't seem to hurt business. Everyone was gathered on the other side, watching the whole thing go down while sipping their drinks.

Officer Brown waved toward the entrance. "She's all yours whenever you want her. Do you need anything else from us?"

"Thank you, Officer. We'll take her from here."

He reached out a hand to stop her. "And you'll keep us updated on what you find?"

Before Rebecca could answer, Darian came back in. More like stormed in. The man moved with so much aggression in every step, he caught the eye of every cop in the room. His shoulders were stiff, his fists clenched tight. Even the barflies shifted uneasily as he stormed past them like a thundercloud.

The pit fell out of Rebecca's stomach. *Dear god, what has he found that put that murderous rage in his eyes? Was it one of the girls? Something worse? Parts of them? Could it be...*

Darian jerked to a halt in front of her. His voice rumbled with anger when he finally spoke. "She has Nugget in a duffel bag stuffed in the trunk."

Relief flooded Rebecca's body, then was strangled as a wave of nausea took its place. Temperatures had been in the mid-eighties since noon. The trunk of a car could easily get over one hundred degrees in this climate. Rebecca slapped her hand over her mouth, struggling to hold down bile as a sensory memory came flooding back. The reek of boiled flesh, waste, and wet upholstery.

"He's only nine weeks old," she managed to force out, swallowing hard.

"Who?" Officer Brown looked back and forth between them. "Did she have another victim in her car? I didn't know she was taking babies."

"He's a puppy." Darian took a deep breath in through his nose. Rebecca had to take a moment, tipping her head back and taking in a cleansing breath herself. "They used him to lure the Harper girl this morning. I pulled him out of the bag and spotted purple and orange chalk smeared on the white in his coat, on his belly."

Officer Brown frowned. "A puppy."

"What kind of sick fuck locks a puppy in a trunk?" Darian turned his glare on Brown.

Brown shook his head and then caught sight of Rebecca, who was trying to regain her composure. "You okay, ma'am?"

Darian thrust a finger toward the door. "A couple of your officers are losing their lunch in the lot right now. It's a bad scene. Animal control is responding with an emergency vet too."

"We need…" Rebecca had to swallow again before she could finish. Ocean air. Wood wax. Citronella oil. *Focus on what you can smell around you. Oh god, I need a cup of coffee.* "Is the puppy dead?"

Darian shook his head and rotated his shoulders. "Barely breathing and not responsive."

With a mental slap, Rebecca pulled herself together. "We need to gather the chalk from his fur and check to see if he's chipped. Full workup as evidence. Make sure the techs get that all gathered. The Carrs got out of this last time on a technicality. We can't let that happen again. All t's need to be crossed and i's dotted."

"I left him with a tech. Right or wrong, they even debated whether they could use alcohol to cool him down like people cool down babies."

At least someone was doing something, unlike Tammy Carr.

"He's a damn puppy." Rebecca was unable to keep the horror off her face. "All that woman had to do was open the trunk and let him run off. Is she such a sociopath that she couldn't be bothered to do even that?"

"There's something else in the trunk too. Clothing tags." Darian reached up to run a hand over his hair, then stopped, his face blanching.

"Your sleeves are saturated." Rebecca gave him a sympathetic smile.

Brown looked at them both again, clearly confused, but he was standing in front of a fan. "The smell?"

Just talking about it made everything worse, and Rebecca gave in. Heading for the bar, she waved the bartender over. Thankfully, he came jogging over and didn't take his time.

"You need something else?"

"We need a bag of ice pronto. Then two glasses of water with lots of ice."

His eyes went wide as he grabbed a trash bag first and tossed several scoops inside. Rebecca took it from him and handed it to an officer standing around. "Take this to the folks working on the puppy."

By the time she turned back around, two glasses filled with ice sat on the bar top. She grabbed them both.

"Toss it back, Hudson," she directed, before taking her own advice.

When she lowered her glass, the bartender refilled it without a word, then filled Darian's as soon as he set it down.

"Now you can sip." Taking a tiny sip, she swirled the water around in her mouth. Now that she was nicely shocked from the cold, she could breathe without thinking of that lingering stench. "I take it you've never opened up a metal box containing a living creature while it sat in the sun, Officer Brown."

He shook his head, his confusion clearing.

"The stench. It's like a miasma. It seeps into everything. There's really nothing else like it in the world. It's sweet and cloying. Thick and wet. And it sticks to everything. It soaks in—"

Darian made a choking sound and knocked back the glass of water again.

"Go get washed up, Hudson. Take your time."

"I was wearing gloves." He stared at his hands as if they'd betrayed him.

Rebecca shook her head. "Doesn't seem to matter. It's in the air, so when you opened the trunk..."

Darian gulped, slammed down his glass, and hurried off to the men's room.

"Aerosolized body, with something that smells like death but is somehow worse. The body is, for lack of a better word, essentially boiled in its own bodily fluids as the air gets supersaturated. There's a cloud of it when you first crack the enclosed space open. When you smell it, you just know that something was cooked alive. If they can do that to a puppy, a creature with no way of identifying them," she turned and stared into Brown's eyes, "they can do it to little girls who can talk."

Brown cursed under his breath. "We gotta take them down."

"We will." Taking another sip of water, she nodded toward the door. "You should go check on your men. Take them some water."

The bartender, who had been listening, dropped slices of lemons into Rebecca's and Darian's glasses. "None of that sounds good. Lemme grab a waitress to take something out to them."

Brown nodded, still frowning. He didn't get it. Unfortunately for him, he soon would. It was his techs who would be tearing apart the car and trunk.

Rebecca fished out one of her lemons and took a bite. The refreshing citrus helped to cleanse her palate, and she felt a wave of relief. Digging her wallet out of her back pocket, Rebecca dropped a ten-dollar bill in the tip jar. Picking up Darian's glass as well as her own, she wandered out onto the patio to get some fresh air.

The outdoor sitting area was lined with pavers, a small fire pit in the middle, and tiki torches marked the edges. It was very much like the one described in the Lynnhaven kidnapping.

Is that how they found their first victim?

Had Tammy Carr been sitting at the bar, drinking, and seen a girl that fit the bill? Or was it a crime of opportunity? Had Rebecca gotten this wrong, and they weren't kidnapping girls to sell? Could there be a different reason for it?

She glanced over at the huddle of police. A couple of them leaned against the wall of the neighboring building, in different stages of hunched-over misery. The techs were walking around with masks on, and she was certain they'd smeared mentholated ointment on their lips or noses. It was about the only way to keep the smell from getting to them.

In the distance, an ambulance siren steadily grew louder. Had someone overreacted to the cops puking, or were they worried about possible hazardous material in the car?

Lifting the lemon water to her lips, she took in the rest of the scene. People walking past and staring. Pedestrians going about their day without even noticing. Traffic driving past as

quickly as they could to get away from the cops. No one wanted to mess up their night by seeing whatever had the cops puking.

Which was why the gray SUV slowly creeping past caught Rebecca's eye.

The passenger window was down, and the driver was leaning over, his eyes roving over the crowd. Without understanding why, Rebecca turned her body, hiding her gun and badge. Stepping back into the shadows, she watched the man scoping the scene.

Was it her paranoia, or was he way too interested in what was happening? He had a creep vibe to him she couldn't ignore.

It's the eyes.

"There you are. I thought you'd walked off and left me behind after I nearly lost it in there."

"Nope, just needed some air. We got lemons. They'll help." Realizing that the SUV driver wasn't the only rubbernecker, Rebecca handed the glass over to her deputy. Paranoia was a hell of a drug. "Coffee cleans your sense of smell, but lemon isn't a bad alternative."

Darian nodded and began drinking his water again. "When life hands you nasty smells, drink lemonade, huh?"

Rubbernecker or not, Rebecca watched the SUV until it turned the corner, pissed that it didn't turn in a way that she could read its plates.

Plucking the lemon she'd already bitten out of her glass, Rebecca crushed it between her palms, grinding them together in order to wring out as much juice as she could.

"As I told Brown after you left, that's one of the worst smells there is. When you mix that with the fact it was a helpless fluffy puppy, it gets real bad. At least for me. I'm a dog person myself. Love dogs. Wanted to get a puppy after I settled down somewhere. That's the plan, at least."

Reaching out, she wiped the backs of Darian's hands with the juice, startling him. He watched her as she coated his skin and the cuffs of his sleeves. "It lingers too. It's been...six years, I think, since I smelled it the first time. Now I can smell it just thinking about it. Sometimes having a good memory isn't a good thing. The lemon will act as a natural deodorizer."

Darian stared at his hands, then at her, searching her eyes. "You had an FBI case with a puppy locked in a trunk before?"

Rebecca shook her head, staring off into the sky. "Not a puppy. A woman. Went missing. She was high profile. And we later learned she was having an affair with a married man. Turned out she'd fallen into a car trunk while loading it up for a weekend getaway with her lover. Was in there for an entire day. Still alive when we found her. She didn't make it."

"You guys didn't think to check her car?" Darian sounded appalled.

"It wasn't her car. It was her boyfriend's. It took us awhile to connect them, then he didn't want to tell us they'd been planning to leave for the weekend and thought she'd been taken before she could show up. He didn't say anything, and he had a solid alibi, so we didn't look for his car at first. Just checked it on a basic follow-up when we realized he was getting a taxi to go everywhere."

Darian shook his head. "A tiny bit of information would have saved her life. Shit."

"Exactly. So how about we see what information we can get out of Tammy Carr?"

"Should be pretty easy, considering the other thing I found in her vehicle." Darian held up his phone, showing her a picture of tags for what appeared to be little girl clothes from a shop called Tiny Treasures. Not evidence-worthy, but enough to help push Tammy, if needed.

"Is that all?"

Darian swiped his screen. "We found this receipt too."

Rebecca zoomed in. The scripty logo at the top was followed by a list containing three dresses, shoes, and tiaras. There was even costume jewelry and a little makeup kit. It was everything a seller might need to turn three little girls into pretty princesses for a night with the twisted assholes ponying up the cash.

Rebecca gritted her teeth, wondering if she could get away with shoving all three of the tiaras up Tammy Carr's ass.

21

Hoyt couldn't help but raise both eyebrows when West came in, pulling along a handcuffed woman with Darian two steps behind. She tossed a thumb drive on the counter and asked Viviane to add the contents to the case folder.

All three of them were a bit green around the gills.

"Sheriff, you got…" Viviane trailed off as West stormed straight through and into the back. "Never mind." Her nose wrinkled. "What's…what's that smell?"

Darian started unbuttoning his shirt and headed straight to Hoyt.

He eyed the younger man up and down. There hadn't been any chatter on the radio except to say they'd found Tammy and Nugget, but Darian looked like he was about to throw up.

Then…something assaulted Hoyt's nostrils.

"What the hell?" He covered his nose with his arm.

Darian shrugged out of the shirt. "I need a favor."

The deputy didn't need to spell it out.

"There's a spare uniform hanging in my locker. I wore it

this morning, but it's got to smell better than whatever's on you." Hoyt's eyes started to burn. The smell was almost putrid, but he couldn't quite place it.

"Thanks. Can you sit in on the interview with the sheriff while I shower?" Darian kicked off his shoes. "If I have to see that bitch Tammy for another minute, I might end up killing her. So might the sheriff."

"Yeah, I can do that. You go get cleaned up." Hoyt shooed him off, then turned to pour a cup of coffee.

Greg, having watched the whole thing, got up from his desk and wandered over. "What was that about?"

Hoyt shook his head. "I have no idea, but he smelled awful."

"Dead bodies? I didn't hear about any."

"No, something worse. Like he'd fallen into a bog, but also worse than that."

"Worse than…? Oh." Greg blanched. "You said they found the puppy?"

"Yeah."

"Locked in a car?" When Hoyt nodded, Greg groaned. "It's been a hot day." Greg went back to his chair, shaking his head. "That poor pup."

Realizing that neither of them had brought back the puppy with them, Hoyt sent up a quick prayer, holding the coffee cup under his nose to clear it. Darian was nearly as much of a dog lover as he was. If Tammy Carr had hurt a puppy, that would explain why Darian was so angry.

Kids and puppies. That was who they were victimizing…

Hoyt took a few deep breaths. He needed to avoid that line of thinking if he was going to be any good in the interrogation room. Darian had asked him to step in because he couldn't handle it. That might have been the first time the man had ever backed down from anything.

I can't let him down.

West came back out and headed directly to Hoyt, an angry and determined look on her face. It wasn't until she was within a couple of yards that Hoyt realized she was actually blowing air out her nose and taking in shallow breaths through her mouth. He held the coffee out to her as an offering. "I haven't even taken a sip yet."

The sheriff grabbed the cup and held it under her nose, sucking in deep breaths through her nose and closing her eyes.

"Heard the pup was locked in a car all day?" Greg ventured. "Must've been bad."

West didn't bother to open her eyes. "It was, and Darian was the one who opened the trunk."

Greg flinched. "He's gone to take a shower and borrow a uniform from Frost."

"Good. Cause the lemons I used on his shirt weren't enough. We had to ride back with all the windows open." She pulled in deep breaths of the coffee steam, seeming to settle down a little bit more with each breath. "Normally, odor receptors stop sending messages to the brain after a few minutes. Not this time."

"Heightened emotion's probably causing you to retain the scent."

Hoyt did a double take at Greg. For an old geezer, he was pretty damn smart. But they were getting way off track. "And now, in order to save three girls, you have to interrogate a woman so evil she locks puppies in trunks. In the summer."

"Yep." Opening her eyes, she glanced back and forth between both men. "Which one of you is going to sit in with me?"

Hoyt glanced over at Greg, but he was already shaking his head. "Nope. Nope. I'll get my ass fired and probably arrested. And sent to Hell along with her. Nope. Had a cat get himself locked in a toolbox one summer, so I have an idea what she did to that puppy."

West lowered the coffee cup. "That's terrible."

"Damn straight it was. If I went in that room, I'd get all the answers out of her, but none would be useable in court." Greg's hands shook as he stood and went for the door. "And if you'll excuse me, ladies, I need to remove myself from this situation right now. I don't want you to see me like this."

Viviane rose from her desk. "What am I missing?"

"She slowly tortured a puppy, nearly to death."

"Tortured?" Viviane dropped back in her seat. "Nugget!"

In his mind's eye, Hoyt remembered the excited, hopeful look on the mom's face as she'd talked about how much her son loved his new puppy. How pleased the family was to know that the police were looking into the case, because she was certain their new dog would be brought home unharmed.

"He's being treated by a vet right now. Hopefully, he'll pull through, but I need you to put that out of your mind. I need you to go into that interrogation room with me and play the good cop. Be the one she can get to empathize with her. Can you make her buy into that?"

Boomer's sweet little puppy face, from when he'd brought her home from the shelter, welled up in Hoyt's mind. She was so tiny, so loving, covering his face with licks and chasing after him everywhere he went. Attacking his shoes. Sleeping at the front door, waiting for him when he got home every day.

A little waggling ball of fluff and love he could cradle in one hand. She was eleven weeks when he'd gotten her. Now she was slow and mostly gray, her eyes had the blue haze of cataracts, and she still followed him everywhere he went. She'd spent every day of his recovery sitting by his bed, keeping an eye on him, and cheering him up.

He took all those warm, loving memories and tucked them away in a box inside his mind where they couldn't be sullied. "Yeah, I can do that. But I'm going home tonight and hugging my dog."

West nodded, her eyes showing she understood completely. "Give your dog an extra squeeze from me." The jealousy in her tone made him smile. Everyone should be jealous of his dog. She was the best.

"Let's do this." He took a deep breath and let it out. "What do we got?"

"An FBI analyst. Let's see what he's come up with." West spun around and finally took a sip of the coffee he'd handed her.

Hoyt followed her back to her office. Oddly, the door was closed. West knocked on it before letting herself in. *Is she worried about spooking the Feebie?*

"Okay, Stalwart, tell me you have something."

"Not a lot, honestly, ma'am." Stalwart wasn't nearly as put together as he had been when he'd arrived. His hair was ruffled, and his jacket was hanging on the back of the hard chair, but he looked a lot more comfortable with his tie loosened and collar undone.

West shook her head. "Give me what you have, and I'll let you know if it's any good."

"Tammy Carr, fifty-two, maiden name Espry, youngest daughter of Anthony and Lorene Espry. Left home at seventeen and moved to Atlantic City, New Jersey. Worked in casinos and bars as a waitress 'til she was twenty-four. After that, no work record."

West leaned closer to the screen. "What else?"

"Married Jon Carr when she was thirty-two. Gave birth to a girl, Adele Carr, six months later. She's filed her taxes every couple of years her entire life, never went so long that she got in trouble. Purchased her home with Jon Carr less than a year after they married. Looks like he was always the breadwinner in the family, not unusual for someone with a young child. No more children after the girl. Also, their child was never enrolled in any schools, doesn't have a vaccination record, no—"

"Is there a death record?"

Stalwart lifted both eyebrows. "For Adele? No. There are records for Tammy's parents, who both died in a car accident. And, get this, Tammy was the sole inheritor, despite leaving home and, as far as I can tell, having no contact with them for the remainder of their lives. But there was a will, presented by Tammy's attorney, that gave everything to her, nothing to her siblings. The estate was so small it wasn't worth fighting over. She sold everything and went back to living her life."

"What about a baptism? For her or Adele? Where was she married?"

"Baptism and catechism for Tammy, none for Adele. They were married in Our Lady Star of the Sea Church."

"Roman Catholic?"

"Yep." Stalwart shot a glance at West, who was taking notes. "Is that helpful?"

"Oh, yeah. What about state assistance? Medicare? WIC?"

"WIC and SNAP, and only for a year."

West nodded as if she'd expected that. "She couldn't keep getting WIC without a baby to show for it."

Hoyt felt his skin go cold. Stalwart just nodded along as if that made sense. Damn, he was glad he'd never gone into the FBI.

"And what did you find on local traffickers?"

"Take your pick. I did a search for each crime scene in this case. Around New Jersey, specifically around Atlantic City where she's from. A Mr. Kevin McGuire." Stalwart motioned at his screen, and West walked around to look.

West made a humming noise as she read. Tapping the screen, the sheriff smiled. "That's the one. This is the guy."

"What guy?" Hoyt was playing catch-up. Something he foresaw becoming commonplace following West's lead.

"The buyer."

"Yeah? How do you know?" Stalwart started clicking around before Hoyt could get around to see who they were looking at.

"Because I saw this piece of shit earlier today driving past the bar where we picked up Tammy Carr." She patted the agent on the shoulder and moved out from behind the desk. "Stalwart, good job. Focus on that scumbag for now."

"Yes, ma'am."

West checked her watch. "I wish we had more time to let her sit in that room and panic, but we don't. We're going to take what you already gave us and go crack the psychopathic bitch. We need to find a way to break McGuire's supply chain apart. And get me every vehicle that's registered to him. Especially if it's an SUV with Virginia plates. And call this in and update the NCIC too."

"On it." Stalwart went right back to his clicking and typing, and Hoyt was left to follow West down to the interrogation room, where the lowlife was waiting.

He'd never been so ready to demolish a suspect.

22

The drunk-ass bitch wasn't answering her phone. That meant Tammy was busy shagging some guy in the alley behind the bar, or the idiot had gotten herself caught. I was betting on the former.

As stupid as she was, she was also sly like a fox and could turn on the charm whenever it suited her. She'd managed to talk her way out of every bad spot she'd ever been in. Over the years, she'd found herself in a lot of dangerous situations, so she had plenty of practice.

Still, Tammy had never screwed up a meetup before. That was what had me on edge. Not only should she have called me by now, but she should've been here already. She was supposed to meet McGuire and bring him down to pick up his merchandise.

Unless she was busy fucking McGuire. That was also something my wife was good at. Using her wares to convince men to go along with her plans. And pissing me off. That was her singular greatest talent.

Unable to take the silence any longer, I went to find Muscles. He'd been skulking around the house like a shark looking for prey. The guy was creepy. Steroids and cocaine will do that to a man.

But he might have some information or a way to contact McGuire to make sure we were still on for tonight. I found him peering through the front windows, right where he could be seen by anyone driving past on the road. What an idiot.

"Shut those blinds before someone sees you. This is supposed to be an abandoned house."

Muscles turned and looked at me. No. He looked *through* me. Yeah, his anchor didn't reach the bottom. "This place is a dump."

I couldn't argue that because he wasn't wrong. I changed the subject instead. "Have you heard from your boss? He's running late. He needs to get here and make the trade, or I'm gonna take the merchandise and find a different buyer."

Muscles didn't react to the question or threat. "He'll be here. I'll call to check his ETA, then we need to douse the girls with the spray."

Without another word, he walked past me and headed for the back of the house. Well, at least he wasn't hanging out in the window anymore. I followed a few steps behind. Muscles walked out the back door, pulling it closed.

Something about this had my nerves on edge. Maybe it was the fact that nothing was going right, but my worry ran deeper than that. I gave it a few more minutes, then walked to the door. I'd installed the peephole years ago. Instead of a regular tube you could peek out of, it was a cone. Like an old-fashioned hearing aid, it funneled all the sounds from in front of the door and channeled it inside.

Muscles was hanging out by the car with his phone to his ear. I pressed my ear against the door.

"You're kidding me. She got picked up where?" A long pause was followed by, "Shit. What do you want me to do?

Yeah, the house is clear. Just him. Packages are ready to move. Okay, yeah, that'll be easy."

The sudden happy tone in his voice made me risk sneaking a glance.

Muscles was smiling as he pulled something from his car. He spun a silencer onto his gun and didn't bother to tuck the weapon away. That meant one thing. He planned to use it soon.

Shit. Things hadn't just gone sideways. They'd gone tits up.

Tammy had gotten picked up, and McGuire wanted me dead. All because of my damn wife. She would rat me out in a heartbeat, and McGuire knew that. He was tying up loose ends. I was the loosest.

Why had I given her my address? Maybe *I* was the idiot.

I only had a few minutes to figure out what to do. I didn't have a gun on me. I didn't even have a weapon. I didn't need a weapon to swipe kids. Just a van and a puppy.

Looking around, I picked up the bottle of beer. At least I hadn't emptied this one yet. Hearing his footsteps move up the porch, I pressed myself flat against the wall next to the doorframe.

The door swung open, and Muscles walked in, gun leading the way. "Hey, man, you got any beer?"

What luck!

He saw me, but not soon enough. I brought the bottle down, catching Muscles on the temple. He'd been about to turn, so when I clobbered him, he lost his balance and fell sideways, his gun arm coming up.

This was my chance.

I snatched the gun and managed to wrench it from his hand. I pulled back, putting as much room between us as possible.

He recovered quickly but froze as I pointed the barrel straight at his head.

I gave myself a moment for my hammering heart to slow before speaking. "Tammy might be out of the picture, but I'm not. Considering you were willing to kill me instead of just cutting and leaving, I'm betting McGuire has buyers he doesn't want to piss off. That works for me. Bring me my money, and you get the girls. Don't bring me my money, and I'll kill all of them and you. And then McGuire can explain why he wasn't able to keep his word. You hear me?"

I couldn't stop my hands from shaking, but my voice was clear as sunshine.

"You don't want to do this."

I snorted. "Sure, I do. Go get me my money. What we agreed on is still fine since I'll be taking Tammy's portion too." I flicked the gun at the goon's head, trying not to look as terrified as I felt. If it had been a fair fight, I would have lost right off the bat. "Think you can remember all that, or should I just shoot you, take your phone, and call McGuire myself?"

Muscles nodded, his eyes never leaving the gun. "I can do that."

"Good. Do it outside." I almost waved the gun at the door, but Muscles tensed up, so I kept the gun trained on him.

I shifted to the side, stepping carefully away from the door so he could walk out without getting close enough to grab me.

Muscles mirrored my actions, walking sideways until he was at the door. "I'll do what you want. Be here when I get back."

"Go. And if you think you can grab another gun, remember that I can kill the girls in a heartbeat. I don't give two shits about them. We all want the same thing here. And tell McGuire to hurry if he wants the girls before the cops find the place. I'm sure he has something that can handle small-town pigs if it comes to it, so tell him to come heavy or not at all."

Muscles took the porch steps backward, keeping his eyes on me.

As soon as he was far enough, I kicked the door closed and threw the lock. That was another thing I'd kept well maintained.

Tammy was probably spilling her guts to the cops already, throwing me under the bus. How long before she gave away my hideout? They would be here any minute.

Moving toward the padded room, I sighed. Those girls were the only card I had left to play.

23

Rebecca's heart rate sped up as she opened the interrogation room door and nodded for Hoyt to enter first.

He let out a long breath and stepped inside. "Good evening, Mrs. Carr." His conversational tone was perfect.

Tammy's eyes followed Hoyt as he moved to sit across from her at the table. Rebecca closed the door and moved to stand against the side wall, staying out of the way.

"Oh, please, that sounds so formal. Call me Tammy. All my friends do." She tried to fluff her hair, but the handcuffs stopped her a few inches short.

Appearing concerned, Hoyt pulled a key from his pocket just like Rebecca had told him to. "Here, let's get these off. I don't want you to be uncomfortable."

Tammy blinked in a flirty fashion. "Why, that's so kind of you."

Hoyt pulled out a winsome smile that turned him from a seasoned cop to a friendly neighbor who'd loan you his power tools in a pinch.

Rebecca wondered if Viviane and Hoyt had learned how

to smile from the same person, deploying the Southern charm like that.

"You're very welcome. No need for all that, is there, Mrs. Carr? We're just trying to have a friendly conversation after all."

"Now, Sheriff. I've already told you to call me Tammy."

Hoyt didn't correct her, which Rebecca appreciated.

"That's a pretty name. So, Tammy, what were you doing at the bar today?"

Tammy didn't even hesitate. "Well, they've just got the best mint juleps."

Hoyt's eyebrows went up. "You know, you're not the only person to tell me that. Have you been drinking mint juleps all day? I could never take more than one or two when it's this hot out. All that mint would tear up my stomach." He patted his belly. "Or maybe that's just because I'm getting up there in years. I'm sure a much younger lady like yourself doesn't need to worry about that."

The compliment was so smooth that Tammy preened. "Sheriff, you're so sweet! But, no, I know better than to drink on an empty stomach. I had a nice juicy burger with slaw and potato planks."

Hoyt licked his lips in an almost indecent way. "That does sound delicious."

Was Hoyt...flirting with this devil woman? Well, that was one way to get information out of a suspect. And Tammy was lapping it up.

"Oh, it was. It was so good, I was thinking about going back for dinner tonight." Tammy leaned forward, putting her breasts on display. She had pulled her top lower since Rebecca had locked her in here. "Maybe you could join me."

A slow smile spread on the deputy's face. "I'd like that. After we get this mess all cleared up."

Tammy waved a hand. "Oh, this business with Jon. It's

always something terrible when his name comes up. The sins of my naïve youth still causing me grief today." Lifting her arms up on the table, Tammy leaned forward even farther. "If I could get the diocese to agree, I would have divorced that man so long ago."

Compassion became a living thing on Hoyt's face. The man was good at this. "I'm so sorry for everything you've been through, Tammy."

She wiped away a fake tear. "Not that he's a bad man, necessarily. Which is probably why the church won't grant my petition. But there's just so much pain between us now. He never recovered after we lost our baby. Started hanging out with a bad crowd. Gambling and drinking. Then there was that awful thing before, with those kids. I never believed it, though. There was no way a man I once loved so much could truly be an abductor. I like to think I'm a better judge of character than that."

The woman was walking a fine line between seductress and disillusioned romantic who needed protection from the harsh truths in life. Rebecca could see how some men could fall for her act.

"That thing being when he was charged with kidnapping?" Hoyt leaned back and opened the folder in front of him, pretending to be reading a file. "Says here they ended up unable to find enough evidence to use against him."

"See!" Tammy tapped her finger on the table. "I was right about him. He's not a bad guy. He just has bad luck. It started when our daughter died." After a dramatic sigh, she wiped a finger gently over her cheek. "And it just hasn't gotten any better."

"I see. You don't think he's involved in the most recent kidnappings that have happened here?"

"Kidnappings?" She patted her ample chest. "I haven't heard of that. Has someone lost their child? Like we did?"

That was strange wording, and Rebecca took note.

"Three children have gone missing in the past week. You can see why we'd be interested in Jon, since he's been charged with this before."

"I told him he needed to get that expunged from his record. Now anytime a child goes missing, the police come knocking. Not that it's not understandable, what with him being accused before."

"So you've talked with him within the last five years, then?"

"What?" Tammy was caught off guard.

"Well, you said that you told him to get his record expunged. That would have to be sometime after the charges against him were dropped." Hoyt glanced down at the folder again.

"Oh, yes. Well, of course I reached out to him. He was so hurt after being accused of such terrible things. I wanted to help him if I could. Just give him some advice, and he had just gotten out of jail and needed some money."

"And a place to stay?" Hoyt glanced up, a hopeful look in his eyes while his tone said he wanted her to deny it.

"Oh, that wouldn't have been right of me. We're not really married anymore. Just on paper. I couldn't take him into my home. I live alone and have since we split." Tammy shifted in her chair, as if the thought made her uncomfortable.

Of course, they'd been sent the video footage of the raid on Tammy's house and knew that there was men's clothing hanging in her bedroom closet. If it wasn't Jon's, then whose was it?

Maybe the guy in the gray SUV? Kevin McGuire.

"Have you been seeing anyone since you and your husband separated?" Hoyt ducked his head shyly. "Sorry, ma'am. That came out wrong."

Tammy reached out with one hand, coming just short of touching Hoyt. "No one serious since then. Not yet."

Hoyt cleared his throat and shifted in his seat. "Um, let's see, um, we don't have any records of where he's been staying since then."

Rebecca nearly smiled, witnessing Hoyt acting like a hormone-fueled teen.

"I'm not really sure." Tammy fluttered her lashes. "It's been so long. I know he's been staying in this area recently, but…"

"Well, if you've been trying to help him get cleaned up, I'm sure you've met him somewhere. Maybe a house he rented? If we can get him in here and talk to him, then we can let you go." He held his pen up, ready to take down notes with an expectant smile on his face.

"Let's see…" Tammy made a show of thinking. Her acting skills were mildly impressive, considering how many drinks she'd had. "There was that place, 1552 Apple Street."

"Apple Street? Do you mean Peach Street? We don't have an Apple Street."

"Oh, Peach Street. That sounds right. I knew it was some kind of fruit."

Hoyt wrote that down while nodding. "Okay, and where else?"

"Where else?"

He looked up and gave her that charming smile again. "Well, we know he wasn't renting a place, so he was probably squatting in more than one house. Most likely, he told you they were short-term leases, or he was house-sitting or something."

"He did tell me he was house-sitting. It was how he made a little money." Tammy nodded. "There was that nice house over on Elm, and another one on Palmer. For a short time, he was staying with friends at the end of Slate. I don't remember any of the house numbers. I'm sorry. It was so very long ago."

"Understandable. Something that isn't important to you emotionally is often forgotten." Hoyt did his teenage shuffle again, shooting a glance at Rebecca.

"See, I knew you would understand, Sheriff."

"Actually," Rebecca pushed away from the wall, "he's not the sheriff here. I am."

Tammy spun to watch Rebecca as she moved closer to the table.

Hoyt pushed back in his chair and stood, his smile falling off his face. Rebecca took the seat, flipping open the folder and laying it flat.

"And, as the woman in charge, I can tell you that there are a lot of holes in your story. The first of which is everything we found in your car. You can be sure we're going to add animal cruelty to the list of charges against you."

Tammy gave a charming, tinkling laugh. "My car? I haven't driven anywhere since I parked it at the bar this morning."

"Then how did you get that burger and potato planks? That bar doesn't serve full meals."

Tammy's pleasant smile faded away, and she glanced up at Hoyt. He ignored her.

"Well, I might have lied about getting the burger. Didn't want this handsome man thinking I was a lush." She gave that tittering laugh again.

"Hmm, well, that doesn't explain how we've got you on camera leaving the parking lot to meet up with your husband. We also have Jon Carr transferring Sylvie Harper from a van to a vehicle within your line of sight. He then placed a puppy used to lure the child into the trunk of your vehicle and took a bag of children's clothing from your vehicle to his. You then drove back to the bar to pick up where you'd left off, hoping to keep your cover story intact. All the while leaving that helpless puppy stuffed in your trunk."

Tammy batted her eyelashes. "I think you've confused me for someone else."

Rebecca started to close the folder but made a show of stopping. "Oh...I have to admire your taste, though. The outfits you selected to transform three terrified little girls into princesses are really pretty. I guess the children need to look their best before you sell them to Kevin McGuire."

Tammy flinched at the name, but she tried to hide it by crossing her arms. "Sell? Dear god, woman, who would even think of such a thing? I bought those dresses for my niece's birthday."

"Your niece? And would that be your brother's daughter, or your sister's?"

Tammy faltered, and Rebecca could practically read her mind. This was information that could be checked. Rebecca bet she didn't even know any of their birthdays. Maybe not even their names.

"Well, neither. She's not technically my niece. She's my goddaughter. I just call her my niece because she's basically family."

"Where was your goddaughter baptized?"

Tammy froze. "What?"

"You're Catholic. That's how you were able to get married in a Catholic church. If you're a godmother, then, of course, you were there to stand in for your goddaughter at her baptism. So where was it?"

"I...I don't remember. I—"

"Speaking of baptisms, where was your daughter baptized?"

Tammy's mouth jerked open, then snapped shut. "I don't see what my daughter has to do with this."

Rebecca shrugged, shuffling through the paperwork in front of her, showing Tammy that it was the story of her life. "Maybe they were baptized at the same church? As a good Catholic, you would, of course, have had your daughter baptized as a baby, right?"

For that, Tammy didn't have any answers.

Rebecca pressed on. "I was just curious because we weren't able to find any record of it. Maybe if it was the same place, that would ring a bell."

Rallying, Tammy pulled herself upright. "I don't want to speak of my dead daughter. And she has nothing to do with whatever reason made you pick me up today."

"I'm not so sure about that. We can't find a death certificate for her. Or a grave. We checked all the local graveyards, and she's not listed as having a plot. Even if you cremated her, she would still need to be buried in sacred ground per your religious beliefs. Maybe you lost her the same way the Harpers lost Sylvie. Did you sell her to the same man? Or have you switched buyers since then?"

"How dare you say such a thing to a grieving mother!" Again, Tammy looked to Hoyt for help.

He was as stone-faced and about as sympathetic as a gargoyle.

"Cut the crap, Mrs. Carr. We're still digging up all the skeletons, or in your daughter's case...missing skeletons." Rebecca leaned forward, getting as close to the woman as the table would let her. "But let me tell you what we do know. You stole a golden retriever puppy, gave it to Jon, and went back to the bar while Jon kidnapped Sylvie out from under her father's nose."

Officially, Rebecca didn't know any of that for sure, but she was willing to toss out theories to see which of them landed. She watched the woman's facial expressions and body language closely.

"Then you went back to pick Jon up from where he dropped off the van. You sat in a car registered under your mother's name while he transferred Sylvie Harper into his vehicle and the puppy into yours. From your trunk, he took a bag of children's clothing. Clothing that you'd already torn the tags off of. We found those tags and the receipt near the *dying puppy*."

Tammy checked her nails. "I don't know what you're talking about."

"You must have been pretty buzzed by then. Sloppy. You left the tags and receipt for those clothes in your trunk and didn't even remember to let the puppy go." Rebecca forced a grin. "You know what makes people sloppy besides alcohol?"

Tammy blew on her nails, but Rebecca noticed that her fingers had begun to tremble. "I'm sure you're going to tell me."

"Confidence. You know what makes people confident?"

The hands dropped into Tammy's lap. "What?"

"Practice."

Tammy's lips twisted into a sneer, but her eyes didn't contain malice. They contained a hint of fear. "I'd like to see a lawyer."

Rebecca spread her hands. "Sure, but that will take time. If we find Sylvie and the two other little girls before they're sold, I'll personally make sure the judge knows you assisted. If those girls are gone, I'll make sure you never get a deal."

"Deal?" Tammy's hand fluttered on her chest. "Honey, I haven't done anything wrong."

"Keep lying, and the deal goes out the window." Rebecca checked her watch. "The puppy in your trunk still had traces of chalk from Sylvie Harper's hands. Who picked the parking lot to meet up in? 'Cause whoever did managed to fuck up big time. They didn't notice the video camera attached to a light pole."

"That idiot!" Tammy pushed away the papers, flinging Hoyt's notepad on the floor along with them as she exploded from her seat. "I told him—" Coming to her senses, she dropped back into the chair. "I'd like that lawyer now."

For a brief second, Tammy's eyes flicked to the notepad, then jerked up to glare at Hoyt.

Rebecca saw it and knew she had what she needed.

"All right. Do you have a lawyer, or shall I call a public defender?" Rebecca picked up the notepad and set it on the table.

"Public defender is fine." Tammy turned in her seat to face the wall.

"That's good. You already dodged all the questions I needed answers to anyway. Thanks for that." Rebecca stood, gathered her things, and left the room. Hoyt closed the door behind them.

"Well, that didn't get us very far." Hoyt swiped at his arms. "Except now I need to take a shower too. That woman is slime."

Rebecca pointed to the list of street names. "We've got these."

He shook his head. "A couple street names. No house numbers."

"She's not as good a liar as she thinks she is. A B-list actress, maybe, but that's about it. She couldn't make up any details. How hard is it to make up a church name? Our Lady of Hope. Easy. But she couldn't do that. All she could make up was a simple story, and then she used distractions."

"I noticed that." Hoyt scratched his jaw. "But after that first slipup, she did name roads that are real roads here."

"Which means she probably saw them or used them. Then let's check 1552 on Elm, Palmer, and Slate."

"You think the house number is real?"

Rebecca lifted a shoulder. "Like I said, she's not good on

the fine details." They stepped into the sheriff's office where Stalwart was still scouring the computer. "Anything new?" Rebecca leaned over his shoulder to peek at the screen.

"Everyone's been updated on the possible McGuire link. FBI is keeping a close eye on all his transportation hubs to see if he has a new shipment. Jon Carr hasn't made any purchases as far as I can tell. So wherever he is, he's using cash. But Tammy Carr did make a purchase for more than thirty dollars today at Paco's Burgers and over a hundred dollars at Tiny Treasures clothing store yesterday."

Hoyt brightened. "Paco's and Tiny's are on Palmer Street."

Rebecca thought for a moment, then leaned over the desk and hit the intercom button. "Viviane, can you send Deputies Hudson and Abner back here if they're available, please?"

"Got 'em both. I'll send them right back."

"Stalwart, are you carrying?"

The FBI analyst jerked his head up. "I, um, well, I am."

"You're going to go with Frost to the Palmer address. Only as his backup and driver. If you run into any issues, call it in. That's your main focus. You see anything, both of you call it in and wait for backup."

As Stalwart jumped up and straightened his clothes, Greg walked in. "You called, Sheriff?"

Darian, his curly hair glistening with water, stood behind him.

"I need you two to check out 1552 Slate Street. That's a possible location where the girls are being held. If you're up to date on the file, you'll see the pictures of our three suspects. Tammy has lawyered up, so keep an eye out for a Kevin McGuire and Jon Carr. McGuire most likely knows we have Tammy. I think I saw him at the bar driving a gray SUV with Virginia plates. Also, check derivations of that address, so anything adjacent to or across from your locations too. I don't care if it's a parked car or a cardboard box. Check it."

Rebecca looked them each in the eyes as she spoke and got nods of understanding in return. "This is a trafficking ring. They're going to be quick to shoot and will kill the kids to make their escape. Keep it quiet. No lights, no sirens, and watch each other's backs. Stay off the radios until it's needed. No chatter. We don't want to draw attention to ourselves after we made a big show of leaving earlier. We don't want anything to give us away. These types of people don't care about human life. They have no qualms about killing cops, so be careful."

"That explains why Trent was left on the bridge all day." Greg's mumbled words were directed over his shoulder to Darian.

Rebecca tried to keep her face still and focus on the details of this case, but a snort from the doorway let her know she'd failed, as normal. "I'll take the Elm location."

"Wait." Darian pushed forward. "Who are you taking with you as backup? Surely not Trent. He's already cost us one sheriff."

Ah, that explains why they started calling me Sheriff... That folder they were passing around must have contained the official report of the shootout, so they know what Trent did and didn't do.

Oh well, too bad for him. The truth always comes out.

"I'm good alone. There's no one else to take. Trent *has* to stay where he is in case the kidnappers make a run for it. And to keep up the ruse that we don't know where they are. If we pull him now, it will show our hand." She held her hand up as four mouths dropped open to protest. "I don't think Elm Street will have anything there. Every town has an Elm. I think she just made it up. It was the first on her list of actual street names."

"Wait. 1552. I don't think Elm goes all the way up to 1552." Greg looked at Hoyt to verify.

Rebecca lifted her hands in a *there you have it* gesture. "See? Most likely, this is one of the fakes. And Peach is clearly a fake since she didn't know that street at all."

Hoyt stepped around her and opened one of the book-shelf drawers. "If you're going alone, at least take this to cover your back." He tossed something at Rebecca.

She caught it awkwardly. From the weight of it, she knew what it was. With a sigh at the reasonable request, Rebecca started undoing the Velcro straps of the bulletproof vest, thankful she'd picked up some for herself and the team.

"If you're not taking backup, at least take spare maga-zines." Hoyt's expression said it wasn't optional. "There's probably some in the armory."

"I've got a spare in my holster, Frost." She met his worried gaze. "I leave the house with my gun clean and the ammo heavy every day."

24

A s Greg had deduced, there was no 1552 Elm Street. Elm didn't make it to the 1500s. Still, Rebecca drove slowly down the street, checking each house before the road ended. There were plenty of houses too. Most of them seemed to be occupied with lights glowing from several rooms. Cars were in driveways and lawns were well maintained.

Turning around, Rebecca headed for Palmer Street to back up Hoyt and Stalwart.

What about other derivations?

Checking to see where she was, Rebecca noticed she was in the 800 block. The houses were starting to look less charming.

Maybe 552? Could Tammy have added a number?

She took it slow another few blocks. Slowing way down, having reached the 500 block, she peered through the dark to find 552 Elm Street. It was an older part of town. Definitely less...maintained. And the lots were a little bigger. More room between neighbors. Considering how tall and decrepit the lawn was at 552, it must have been abandoned for awhile.

The house was dark. But wait…

Focusing on the front porch, she saw movement.

All her instincts kicking in, Rebecca reached for the radio as she pulled into the drive, her lights raking over the front porch where a man was sitting. If she left now, that would be even more suspicious.

"Dispatch, checking a suspicious house at 552 Elm Street. Got movement." She threw the cruiser in park, and stepped out, leaving it running, and adjusted her vest to sit properly.

"Can I help you, Officer?"

She could barely see him—just a silhouette of a man against the dark house. The last thing she wanted was to spook him if he was involved in this case.

"We've had calls about a feral dog in the area. It might be rabid. Have you seen anything?" Just to be safe, Rebecca stayed behind the door of the vehicle and unsnapped her holster.

"No dogs here. No barking either. Think I might've seen a bitch or two earlier, though." The man hopped down from the porch into the grass and weeds.

Rebecca forced a smile into her voice. "Rabid dogs don't bark. That's part of what makes them so dangerous. You might want to go inside for the night, either way. It's a chocolate lab mix, so he'd be hard to see in the dark."

"Can't do that." The man laughed. "My old lady caught me texting her sister. I'm safer out here with a rabid dog than I would be inside with her right now."

Rebecca's heart was a hammer in her chest. "I know how that can go. Would you like me to call for backup so we can get you safely back inside? Maybe have a talk with your wife? What's her name?"

"Nah, don't worry about it. I've already called for backup." He was already a quarter of the way through the yard, staying just outside the cruiser's headlights.

A chill worked its way down Rebecca's spine as the sound of a car on the road drew closer. Was that her backup or his?

"Sir, I'm going to need you to stop."

Another laugh. "No, Officer, I think I'm good."

Rebecca pulled her gun. "Sir, put your hands over your head and stay where you are!"

The approaching car was almost in the driveway. The man didn't even slow his steps.

"But there could be a rabid dog out here. What if I'm attacked while my hands are up?"

He was definitely taunting her now. Or trying to distract her.

The car pulled up, and she glanced over her shoulder. It was an SUV with its headlights pointed straight at her, destroying her night vision and blocking any view of the driver.

Shit. She was in trouble.

Rebecca shielded her eyes with her left hand, keeping the gun pointed to her right, doing her best to keep both threats in her peripheral vision. "Shadow Island Sheriff's Department. Show me your hands."

The vehicle shook as the driver stepped out. A burst of rapid-fire gunshots peppered the door next to her. Rebecca was rocked backward as she took a hit.

"Fuck!"

Taking a knee, Rebecca shot at the spot she expected her assailant's head to be.

He cursed.

But she didn't think he'd taken a hit. It was impossible to see, with the headlights pointed right at her. Squinting to see as best as possible, Rebecca directed her next shots at the headlights, knocking them both out.

Footsteps slapped against the dry grass of the yard. The first man was coming up behind her, but she couldn't see him. Did he have a gun? She didn't think so, or he'd most likely have already taken a shot.

With few options available, Rebecca dropped to the ground and rolled under her vehicle. The top of her head brushed against the cruiser's hot frame.

Lifting the radio to her lips, she pressed the button. "Shots fired. 552 Elm. Officer hit."

Her shoulder burned, but she was pretty sure her vest had taken the bullet. With her adrenaline pumping as fast as it was, she couldn't be certain and had zero time to check. Twin circles blotted her vision, creating a kaleidoscope of light as she peered into the darkness and prayed for her night vision to kick in.

Headlights bobbing as the SUV raced toward her.

The screams of a man dying, pinned between two cars.

Pain tearing into her shoulder, her gun hand useless.

Blood on linoleum.

Rebecca dragged the edge of her hand over the sand-covered asphalt of the driveway, centering herself in the here and now. Pushing away the images of her past, she focused on ensuring she'd have a future.

"We're on our way, Rebecca." Hoyt's quiet voice came from her radio.

Listening beyond the engine just above her, Rebecca strained to hear footsteps or any sound that would clue her into her adversaries' locations. The back tire came into focus as her vision cleared.

It was the closest bit of cover between her and the second man. He was the biggest threat, so she was forced to put all her focus on him.

Crawling to the back tire using only her feet and forearms, Rebecca prayed she was making the right decision… and waited.

A leg appeared around the SUV's open door.

Come on, you bastard.

His other leg appeared. When he cleared the door, Rebecca steeled every ounce of courage she possessed and rolled from underneath the cruiser.

As his gun came down to take aim, she shot him in the chest.

His body hit the ground beside her, and when he lifted his gun again, she put another round through his head. With no time to celebrate, she took stock of the situation.

Her Springfield Armory 1911 held seven rounds.

Miss, headlight, headlight, chest, head. Two bullets left in this mag.

A man's voice called out from her right. She twisted. She couldn't make out what he was saying through the ringing in her ears, but she knew it wouldn't be polite conversation.

The man from the porch stepped into the glow of her headlights, and they glinted off the knife in his hand. From this angle, she couldn't tell if he knew where she was, but she wouldn't take any chances.

"Drop your weapon!"

When he took a step her way, Rebecca pulled the trigger twice in rapid succession. One in the chest and one in the neck.

As he dropped to his knees, she reached into her cobbled-together duty belt and pulled out a spare magazine. *Thank you, Angie.* Slapping the fresh mag in place, she rolled to her feet, keeping her weapon raised on the man down. She kicked the knife under the cruiser before turning in a full circle.

Were there more of them sneaking up on her right then?

Staying low, she crept to the passenger door of the SUV, racking the slide as quietly as she could. Popping up, she swept the cab that was lit up from the cabin light. It was empty.

Thank God.

Rebecca blew out a relieved breath but kept a careful check on her surroundings as she went over to the driver. She wasn't surprised to recognize Kevin McGuire. Two fingers at his neck confirmed what she already knew. He was dead.

"Shit."

That meant a crap ton of paperwork, but more than anything else, a dead man couldn't tell her how many children he'd taken over the years. Or where they currently were.

Forcing that realization from her mind, she crept over to the man from the porch and felt for a pulse. Nothing.

Back at the cruiser, she stretched under it and fetched her radio. Her hearing was starting to return as the ringing faded, and she could hear the pounding of her own heart.

"Dispatch, two men down. Send a bus."

"Rebecca, are you okay?" Viviane's voice was filled with worry.

"I think so. I..." She stopped talking as a new sound filled the night air.

"Rebecca, hold on." It was Darian. "We're five minutes out."

Five minutes could mean the difference between life and death for three little girls.

"I'm going in."

"Rebecca! Sheriff!" She barely recognized Hoyt's voice. He was yelling so loudly. "We'll be there in a few minutes."

She didn't have a choice. Racing for the house, Rebecca

watched every shadow to make sure she wasn't running into a trap. She put the radio to her lips one more time.

"I can hear the girls. They don't have five minutes."

25

Rebecca was running full speed as she jumped onto the porch. Peering in through the windows did no good, as they were completely covered from the inside. She listened harder. The screams were coming from the back, farther into the house. Nowhere near the front door.

Turning the knob, she cursed to find it locked. Bracing on her back foot, Rebecca kicked, slamming her heel into the door just to the side of the doorknob. The door gave slightly but stayed closed. She kicked it again, and the door finally broke open. As it swung inward, she fell onto her forward leg, dropping into a crouch, her gun raised and ready. "Sheriff's department! Come out with your hands up!"

There was no answer, and the screams grew louder. They were cries of fear, not pain, but that held little consolation.

Rebecca shuffled forward, wishing she had someone at her back. She'd even take Trent Locke at this point.

"This is the sheriff. Jon Carr, come out with your hands up."

No response other than unrelenting sobs and mumbled words.

Moving as fast as possible, Rebecca cleared the room before heading to the only doorway on the main floor. The cries grew louder with every step she took.

One. Two. Three.

Rounding the doorway, she swept what appeared to be a den. It looked empty. She checked behind everything that could hide a person to confirm before moving toward the light coming from the back.

Moving fast, Rebecca stepped around the doorway. Peeking into a dingy kitchen, she spotted her target.

Jon Carr was crouched in the corner with all three girls in front of him as living shields. He held Sylvie Harper and Emma Bright in place by gripping their hair in one fist. His other hand held a gun under Chelsea Dixon's chin.

All three girls wore their Tiny Treasures dresses. She could see the strap of Sylvie's pony swimsuit peeking out of her collar. As they stared at Rebecca, their screams trailed off to whimpers and sobs.

Rebecca shivered. These children were only minutes—maybe seconds—away from being lost into the world of sex trafficking.

"Jon, drop your weapon."

"I'm not going to jail." He shook his head violently. "Let me go. Put your gun down so I can leave. Once I'm safe, I'll leave the girls behind unharmed."

Rebecca raised her left hand. "Sorry, Jon, I can't do that. I can't let you leave here with these kids. They need to go back to their families."

His hand jerked.

She could see his finger tightening on the trigger. She had to calm him down before he started a series of events that would end up with dead bodies.

Blood on linoleum.

Blood on the cupboards.

Mom...

Stop!

Her mind flashed back to everything Tammy Carr had said about her husband in the newspaper article. She needed to say something that resonated with him.

"Jon, you don't have to keep this up. We already figured the whole thing out. We know what your wife did to you."

Jon stilled. "What she did to me?" He sounded confused, which wasn't good, but it was better than trigger happy. "You know she sold our daughter?"

Rebecca froze, stunned to her core. She hadn't been expecting that admission at all.

Taking a deep breath, she forced herself to focus. She would learn what had happened to Adele after she got these little girls out of this deadly situation.

Her arm was starting to burn with the strain of holding the gun perfectly still.

Right arm useless, can't lift my gun.

Can't protect myself.

They're coming.

Rebecca rolled her shoulder, feeling the vest slide around, a reminder she wasn't in that parking garage. It pissed her off that the events in D.C. held her mind hostage. She just hoped it wouldn't become Shadow's captive too.

"We've already arrested Tammy. We know she was the one who stole the puppy and abducted the children." The lies rolled easily off her tongue. "This is just like the last time, isn't it? When she took those kids and placed the blame on you. But this time, she wised up and had you taking care of them for her, didn't she? Did she even tell you who these kids are, or did she just dump them on you and ask you to watch them? I'm sure with you living in this abandoned house, you probably needed the babysitting money for food, didn't you?"

Jon's eyes widened, and his hand started to tremble. "Yeah." He swallowed and glanced down at the kids.

Rebecca prayed that he'd believe her lies and think he could get away with this if he played his cards right.

"I know she sent those men to kill you, but you're safe now. You're all safe. I'm the sheriff, and I shot the men who were coming here to kill you. They're both dead, so you don't have to worry about them anymore."

"Really?" Jon's voice vibrated like a snake's hiss.

"Really. If you put the gun down and show me that you're not a threat to these little girls you've been taking care of, then you'll be safe. McGuire and his man are dead. There wasn't anyone else here threatening you, was there?"

Jon seemed to be thinking through his options. His hand dropped slightly as he started to calm down. Little Chelsea's chin quivered as the barrel moved away from her skin.

"That's right. Drop the gun. It's obvious that you were trying to protect the girls. Once we get these girls out safe, you can give me your statement and tell me how Tammy tricked you. I bet that's not even your gun, is it, Jon?"

It was a guess, and she was relieved when he shook his head.

"No. I hate guns. I was trying to protect the girls. There was this guy. Really big with lots of muscles. He was going to kill me. This is his gun. I hit him with a beer bottle and took it off him." He laughed as he relived the memory.

"That was smart of you. Using whatever resources available to protect yourself. Whatever you had to do was in self-defense. And it's not like he can press charges against you anyway." Rebecca grimaced and nodded toward the front yard. "He's not exactly in a position to give a statement about anything. Neither of them."

Jon started to lower the weapon but froze as the sound of sirens joined the children's whimpering. "Who—"

"Jon, those are my deputies. If they come in and see their sheriff facing off with a man holding a gun, they're going to shoot first and not ask questions ever."

His eyes darted behind her, as if seeking out the deputies she'd warned him about. "Keep them out."

"I'll try, but they did just lose their sheriff, you know. I'm the new one. They'll do anything they can to not lose their new sheriff so soon." Rebecca smiled at him. "How about we both lower our guns and send the girls out? That way, they'll know everything's under control in here."

Jon swallowed hard and looked down at the children. "Yeah, if I send the girls out, they'll know I'm not involved in this. I was just babysitting for Tammy and didn't know any better until they tried to kill me...yeah."

His arm went lax, and Chelsea's little body swayed away from him. Rebecca wanted to sigh in relief, but it was too early for that.

The siren cut off. "Sheriff! Where are you?" Hoyt's tone was frantic.

"I'm chatting with Jon Carr. Stand down!" She smiled at Jon and held out her free hand. "I won't be able to keep them out for long. Give me the gun that you had to take to defend yourself, and let the girls go."

Rebecca didn't breathe as she watched a thousand emotions cross Jon Carr's face.

"Yeah." Jon lowered the gun to his side. "Go on, girls. Go tell the police about how I kept you safe from the scary man who threw a rat at you."

As soon as he released them, all three girls ran straight at Rebecca. As much as she wanted to scoop them into her arms, she needed to get them to safety.

"Run out the front door, okay? My deputies are there to help you."

"Come on." It was Sylvie. She held out her hands to the others. "Let's get out of here."

"The girls are coming out!" Rebecca shouted after them, keeping her eyes on Jon as he finally set his gun on the floor.

"This is almost over, Jon. Once I walk you out, everyone can be told the truth about what happened tonight and all those years ago."

"Good. Good." Color was returning to Jon's face. "It'll be good to finally clear my name. It's been so hard living with this over my head. That's why I've been homeless." He wiped his palms on his pants, then turned around without being asked, putting his hands behind his back. "Don't want anyone to think I'm a threat. Cops can get cagey in situations like this."

"Good thinking, Jon. That's very smart." Rebecca kicked his gun away before closing the metal cuffs around his wrists. Only after the second one clicked shut did she allow herself to take a deep breath.

"Now we can walk out safely, and you can give your statement."

"Do you believe me?" Jon's voice trembled.

Not a chance, asshole.

"Yes, of course."

They stepped out onto the front porch just as Darian and Greg pulled up. Hoyt stood just off the porch, pointing his gun at her and Jon. Stalwart was loading the girls into their cruiser.

"It's okay!" Jon called out. "Your boss took down the bad guys, and we saved the girls."

Rebecca grinned as Hoyt rushed up to join her, giving her a quizzical stare. She shook her head in an *I'll tell you later* gesture and handed their prisoner over to her deputy.

26

"That's a great picture!" Rebecca leaned over, pretending her shoulder wasn't killing her while handing over a cup of hot cocoa.

Sylvie frowned down at her drawing. "It's a cheeseburger, but it's not in paradise anymore."

Poor kid. She'd drawn a green-and-black burger in what could only be described as a child's version of Hell.

Rebecca wrapped an arm around the girl, who looked so tiny in the hospital bed. "That's just a detour. It doesn't mean the cheeseburger has to stay there, you know?"

Sylvie didn't look convinced but nodded anyway. "So maybe it can go back to paradise some day?"

"Absolutely. It can go wherever you want it to go because it's safe now." Rebecca squeezed her a little harder, forcing herself not to wince. "You understand?"

Sylvie sipped her cocoa. "I think so. It's safe because of you."

Tears burned the backs of Rebecca's eyes. "Safe because of me and a whole bunch of other people, especially your mom and dad. They were ripping the world apart to find you because they love you very much." She forced a smile into her voice. "They may never let you out of their sight again."

A little giggle followed. Not much of one, but enough to lighten Rebecca's heart a bit. "How's Emma and Chelsea?"

What a brave, strong child, thinking of the other girls too.

"They're drinking hot cocoa too and waiting for their parents."

Rebecca didn't tell Sylvie that she was more worried for the other children. They'd been held captive for longer and were more traumatized by their ordeal. Physically, the girls were dehydrated but in overall good condition...physically. Time would tell how well they would do mentally and emotionally.

"That's good. And the bad men?"

Rebecca pressed her lips to the girl's soft hair. "They're in jail now, honey. They can't hurt you or anyone else anymore."

"Sylvie!"

The girl's head snapped up, and she nearly spilled her cocoa at the sound of her mother's voice. Rebecca took the cup and stepped out of the way while the Harpers descended on their daughter.

As hugs and tears filled the room, Rebecca inched toward the door.

"Sheriff?"

Rebecca turned just as Joseph Harper wrapped her in a tremendous bear hug. Trying not to spill the cocoa or curse from the pressure on her shoulder, she hugged him back.

"Thank you," he said when he finally pulled away.

With a heart that swelled with emotion, Rebecca smiled at the entire family. "I'm so happy to see you all together again."

And she was.

She stayed at the hospital long enough to witness each family reunite…then desk duty.

Not because of her minor injury, but because she'd been in an officer-involved shooting.

Her vest had taken the bullet, but she still had a hell of a bruise. At least this time, it was her left shoulder, so it wasn't as limiting. Hoyt had checked her out at the scene and then shot her a knowing grin as he'd shown her the bullet lodged in the vest he'd insisted she put on.

Hours later, Rebecca was the one chilling at the station on administrative leave while her deputies maintained the scene. After shooting two men, she'd relinquished her gun to Hoyt and left him in charge while she rode with the girls away from the chaos. They'd seen enough to last a lifetime.

By midnight, word came that the girls had been reunited with their families and no substantial injuries had been inflicted on them.

By two, Rebecca was climbing into her bed after a long hot shower. They'd also gotten word from the vet that the puppy was stable and was expected to make a full recovery.

By five, Rebecca knew she wasn't going to get any sleep tonight. Her mind wasn't just on the case they'd just solved but on another child. Little Adele. How could any parent sell their child like that?

Rebecca had already put out feelers to see if there might be even the slimmest possibility of finding Adele, but in her heart, she knew it was useless. She wouldn't give up hope quite yet, but neither would she tie herself to the sinking ship of expectation. Adele, if alive, would be a grown woman by now. The reality of that was almost unbearable.

Knowing how futile it was to keep trying, Rebecca got up and pulled on a tank top and shorts. Dawn was still a distant hope, just barely pushing back the dark of night. The dew rose thickly as she stepped out on her back deck and made her way down to the beach. Walking was the only thing that helped on nights like this, as there was no all-night gym on the island.

Nothing beat a walk in the sand. At least while it was warm. *This breeze has got to be brutal in the winter. Will I ever know what that's like?*

Staring into the endless black of the ocean, with only the wind and the waves to keep her company, Rebecca tried to think that through. Winter was a long way away. She'd only had enough money to rent this place for three months, but that had been before she'd started pulling in a paycheck.

Now she could afford the rent for at least a few more weeks beyond that. Enough to extend her vacation by another month. If she ever started it. There were at least two more weeks of paid time for her too. Then, of course, even more weeks would be tacked on while she testified in court.

That realization pulled Rebecca down a different train of thought.

Two major crimes in the two weeks since Alden Wallace had first knocked on her door.

For such a small island, how was that possible?

Cassie Leigh had been murdered, and then this case of child trafficking. How many other girls were being hurt on Shadow Island that Rebecca knew nothing about?

Serenity McCreedy was a perfect example, but the girl refused to give testimony. Her case was essentially closed. After she'd nearly been killed by the same man who'd killed her best friend, Rebecca wasn't about to push her.

Something strange was going on here, but it was nothing she could nail down. Nothing was recorded anywhere. Like the Yacht Club. Wallace had turned a blind eye, and he'd paid for that. She wasn't sure why. But she also didn't think he understood how dangerous it could be to ignore that sort of thing.

Once word got out that the police would turn a blind eye, more criminals would move into an area. The same way hikers talked about where the best trails were, criminals talked about the best places to work their trade.

Bobbing lights in the distance had Rebecca's heart racing before she realized she wasn't hallucinating or stuck in a flashback. They weren't headlights racing toward her.

Someone was running down the beach with a headlamp strapped to their head, a dog keeping pace beside them. She watched them as the light bobbed up and down, growing brighter. Then it steadied and stopped.

"Rebecca?"

Though she couldn't see him, she recognized the voice. "Ryker? Is that you?" The dog cocked his head and wandered her way.

"Yeah, it's...hold on." He pulled the headlamp down around his neck. It lit up his face. "Sorry about that. What are you doing up this early?"

Rebecca came dangerously close to giggling. From the way the shadows fanned up his face, Ryker looked like he was about to tell her a ghost story.

"I haven't actually been to bed yet. Just got home."

"Oh, right." His tawny eyes almost seemed to darken. "That little girl who was kidnapped. But you found her, didn't you?"

"And another two. Yeah. It's been a long day." Ryker's chocolate lab pushed against her knee, vying for her attention. Rebecca squatted down at his level. "Hey there, Humphrey, how are you?"

On hearing his name, Humphrey jumped up, knocking Rebecca on her rump.

"No. Down, boy. Humphrey! Down." Ryker did his best to reel in his overly affectionate dog.

"It's okay." Rebecca laughed, burying her face in the dog's soft fur as she tried not to fall flat on her back.

"This is why I take him out on long runs at dawn. If I don't work this energy out, he'll be insane all day."

"Oh, I get it. And to be blunt, after that last case, I'm due some puppy cuddles." The dog's wet tongue caught Rebecca's lips, and she grimaced. "Yuck. Cuddles, not kisses."

Ryker sank down beside her and pushed a hand through his sandy blond hair. "You've got to be exhausted. This wasn't the best start to your new job out here, but at least it turned out well. Maybe things will settle down now, and you can see what it's really like to be a sheriff like Wallace."

Rebecca's heart squeezed. She didn't want to know what it was like to be a sheriff like Wallace. That thought felt so disrespectful, and she would never voice it out loud, but it was true. Hell, she'd never wanted to be a sheriff at all. Today was the day she'd planned to turn in her badge.

Sheriff was a political appointment just as much as it was a law enforcement position. And she was never very good at politics. Mostly because she hated it.

Her silence lasted too long, but she couldn't think of anything to say.

Ryker did it for her. "It was a rough day for you, wasn't it?"

There was so much sympathy in Ryker's voice, she could only nod.

"I'm sorry. You wanna talk about it?"

She opened her mouth to say no, but other words came flooding out. "It brought back a lot of old memories. Things I came here to deal with, but I keep getting sidetracked."

Ryker ran a hand over the dog's back. "That sounds awful. Can you take a few days off? You've been working nonstop since you started. You deserve to relax."

Rebecca laughed. She was supposed to have three months off.

"Well, I don't have much choice because I'm on admin leave for the next couple days. I might just sleep the whole time."

Ryker nodded and stood, holding a hand down to her. "We'll get out of your hair, then. And off your lap. C'mon, Humph."

Rebecca accepted his help and stood. His hand felt warm in hers. "Thanks. I think I can finally get to sleep now."

"Sleep well, and from a resident of Shadow Island, thanks for everything you've done for us. I hope today will be better."

Rebecca wasn't sure if it was the lamp pointed at his face or the cheesy line, but Ryker's cheeks were red as he turned to continue his run.

Brushing the sand and fur off her legs, she stared at the ocean. As cheesy as it was, it was still nice to get a thank-you. Or maybe it was Humphrey who'd made her feel better. Either way, as the sun finally started to shed light onto the horizon, some of the tightness Rebecca had carried for the last twenty-four hours began to dissipate.

It was a new day. It didn't matter that she hadn't slept yet. Or that Nugget was still at the vet. Or that the girls were safely reunited with their parents.

The sun would always come up the next day. Time kept marching forward.

What did her future look like?

Rebecca had no idea.

27

The day had finally come.

Alden Wallace was laid to rest with all the pomp and love Shadow Island could whip together. It was a Tuesday, and several businesses had closed so the staff and owners could attend the funeral. Even Rebecca was able to join.

She'd officially been taken off leave after the shootings had been deemed justified. Truth be told, she'd been worried about her decision to shoot the man with the knife. But when they'd learned his identity and reviewed his rap sheet, any doubt had been laid to rest.

Wallace's brother sat in the front row and gave a touching eulogy. So did quite a few others. Trent, Darian, and Hoyt all sat in the second row, right behind Tom Wallace.

After the funeral, there was a slow procession to the grave site. Anyone who hadn't made it to the ceremony seemed to be lined up on the street to the cemetery. An honor guard of sorts also lined the roads. Cruisers from neighboring PDs were parked here and there, with officers in plain clothes and deputies saluting the hearse.

After the graveside service, there was the usual slow walk away. People broke into groups, some leaving immediately, others lagging behind to talk.

It was all incredibly touching, but Rebecca couldn't help but feel like the odd woman out. She didn't really know anyone and felt like she was intruding on their grief.

Just as she was about to slip away, Meg Darby walked up to her. Viviane was nowhere in sight, but an older gentleman walked next to her. "There you are, dear."

Rebecca hated moments like these. She was never sure if she should reach her hand out to shake or open her arms to hug or what. What she ended up doing was inclining her head in a respectful nod.

"Rebecca, this is my husband, Dale. Dale, this is the new sheriff I was telling you about."

Feeling a little unsure about being called the "new sheriff," Rebecca still reached out to shake the man's hand when he offered it.

"Good to meet you. And good to have some fresh blood in the department. I can't wait to see what you'll end up doing."

Meg nodded, seemingly just as sure as her husband that not only was Rebecca going to stay on as the sheriff but do a good job as well. It wasn't like Rebecca could deny the position while literally standing at Wallace's graveside.

Before she could respond, Meg continued. "Since you're new here, I thought I'd let you know that there's a post-funeral get-together. It's not formal or anything. In fact, most folks will go home and change into beachwear before joining. We just like having a get-together after a funeral, to celebrate life after laying our friends and loved ones to rest. I made my peach cobbler."

"And the mayor set his grill up this morning," Dale added,

with a pat on his belly. "So you know he's going to have a barbecue."

Meg squeezed Rebecca's arm. "Join us, and don't worry about bringing anything. There'll be plenty."

Rebecca was touched by the invitation. "I'd like that."

Meg beamed at her. "See you in about a half hour then."

As Rebecca watched them walk away, she second-guessed her decision.

Most of Rebecca didn't want to go, but the idea of barbecue and homemade peach cobbler had decided for her. While she'd managed to do a grocery run during her administrative leave, she knew her pantry couldn't compete with either of those delicious treats. Besides, food always tasted better when someone else prepared it.

First things first, though. She needed out of this dress.

Thirty minutes later, she'd changed into her trusty khakis and navy polo shirt. Strapping on her donated duty belt, she was ready to officially report back to duty. She'd run the station so the other deputies could enjoy the evening.

But first…peach cobbler.

Even if Rebecca hadn't known where to go, she could have found the location by following the steady stream of cars and people. And the sound of laughter.

Rebecca made her way into the gathering, maneuvering between people on blankets or in camping chairs and around coolers filled with sodas and beer. She followed her nose to the long tables being set by a line of children carrying dishes. As she approached, she could hear Hoyt talking.

"Then he looks at me and says, 'Well, looks like you're going to be getting overtime pay this week. Congrats!' Then he just walks off and heads home." The crowd gathered around Hoyt burst out in laughter, and she wished she'd gotten here sooner to hear the beginning of the story. "Alden almost never pulled rank, but when he did, I knew it was gonna be messy. Here's to you, Alden. I never did get that stain off my shoes, you bastard." Hoyt lifted a bottle of beer as everyone burst into laughter again and joined him.

Spotting a long-haired collie lying at his feet, Rebecca made her way over.

"Hey, there, Sheriff, did you come to—"

"Well, hey there, girl. You must be Boomer. I've heard so much about you!" Rebecca knelt and held out her hand to the collie, who was looking up at her with friendly eyes and upright ears. Boomer leaned forward and snuffled Rebecca's hand. "Oh, yeah, you're a good girl."

"I don't think she's come over for you, Hoyt." Someone in the crowd laughed.

Rebecca didn't look up. "I can't get away from this guy... see him all the time. But this is my first time meeting this lovely lady."

Boomer wagged her tail and crawled closer to Rebecca, leaning into the scratches, her hind leg starting to thump.

"Do we have money in the budget for a K-9 position?" Rebecca laughed as Boomer rolled over to get some belly rubs. "She's so sweet, we could set her up as an emotional support dog."

"No, she's only my emotional support." Hoyt groused but handed over the leash to her. "But you can borrow her for a little bit while I get another drink."

Rebecca took his vacant chair. "Take your time. This might take awhile."

Boomer leaned her head against Rebecca's knee, rolling her eyes in ecstasy as Rebecca continued scratching her.

"Well, I'm damn glad you're here, Sheriff West."

Rebecca glanced up. It was a woman she didn't know.

"We all loved Wallace, and he was a good man. I voted for him every time. But after the way you've handled things, I'll happily vote for you at the next election."

Not sure what else she could do, Rebecca smiled and thanked her as graciously as she could.

"Maybe you can figure out what's going on with that Yacht Club too. I feel a lot safer having someone with an FBI background looking into things. It's organized crime, dammit. And, well, I'd just feel better with you at the wheel."

"My brother was devoted to his community and job." As Tom Wallace waded in to defend his brother, a few people started looking uncomfortable. "I know he was worried about a group of criminals moving into the area. I never knew what they were called. He said they were some kind of club. I thought he meant bikers. I'm assuming that's the club you're talking about now?"

He glanced around the crowd, and a few people nodded. Rebecca watched it all happen, not sure what would happen next. It was incredibly awkward.

"My brother was a wise man. He knew he was in over his head." Tom looked around at the crowd again.

Rebecca saw he wasn't angry.

"But he also didn't know who he could reach out to for help. He said every time he thought he'd made progress, something would go wrong with the case, and nothing would be done. One man can only do so much when there's a system and a team of lawyers determined to keep him quiet."

A jolt ran through Rebecca. It was nearly the same thing she'd heard from her father. That was why he'd retired from his job. And it had all turned out to be true. She'd learned this when she'd tracked down his killers and unraveled the conspiracy against him.

Had the same thing happened with Wallace? Was it the case of a good man fighting against an organization he didn't understand? Or a cop who'd looked the other way while rich men committed crimes? Rebecca had no way of knowing.

They hadn't known each other long enough for her to begin to measure the kind of man he was.

"Maybe." Tom turned his eyes to Rebecca. "My brother's successor used to be FBI. She can use what she knows to finally wrap up this old case, as she did with this last one."

Rebecca ran her fingers deep in Boomer's fur to keep them from trembling. "Maybe I can."

Maybe I can.

But did she want to?

It wasn't like she didn't know how these things worked. Or the games lawyers and judges played in courts. If Wallace was hitting a brick wall that he didn't know how to circumnavigate…

"Hey, Boss." Hoyt crouched down beside her, his voice low. "You're off leave as of this morning, right?"

Rebecca sighed. "Right." She was afraid to ask but knew she had to. "Why?"

"Because we've got a dead body."

The End
To be continued…

Thank you for reading.
All of the *Shadow Island Series* books can be found on Amazon.

ACKNOWLEDGMENTS

How does one properly thank everyone involved in taking a dream and making it a reality? Here goes.

In addition to our families, whose unending support provided the foundation for us to find the time and energy to put these thoughts on paper, we want to thank the editors who polished our words and made them shine.

Many thanks to our publisher for risking taking on two newbies and giving us the confidence to become bona fide authors.

More than anyone, we want to thank you, our readers, for sharing your most important asset, your time, with this book. We hope with all our hearts we made it worthwhile.

Much love,

Mary & Lori

ABOUT THE AUTHOR

Mary Stone

Mary Stone lives among the majestic Blue Ridge Mountains of East Tennessee with her two dogs, four cats, a couple of energetic boys, and a very patient husband.

As a young girl, she would go to bed every night, wondering what type of creature might be lurking underneath. It wasn't until she was older that she learned that the creatures she needed to most fear were human.

Today, she creates vivid stories with courageous, strong heroines and dastardly villains. She invites you to enter her world of serial killers, FBI agents but never damsels in distress. Her female characters can handle themselves, going toe-to-toe with any male character, protagonist or antagonist.

Discover more about Mary Stone on her website.
www.authormarystone.com

Lori Rhodes

As a tiny girl, from the moment Lori Rhodes first dipped her toe into the surf on a barrier island of Virginia, she was in love. When she grew up and learned all the deep, dark secrets and horrible acts people could commit against each other, she couldn't stop the stories from coming out of the other end of her pen. Somehow, her magical island and the darkness got mixed together and ended up in her first novel. Now, she spends her days making sure the guests at her beach rental cottages are happy, and her nights dreaming up the characters who love her island as much as she does.

Connect with Mary Online

facebook.com/authormarystone
goodreads.com/AuthorMaryStone
bookbub.com/profile/3378576590
pinterest.com/MaryStoneAuthor